SWEET BABY

SUGAR BABIES #3

CHARITY PARKERSON

--Warning: This book is intended for readers over the age of 18.

Copyright © 2019 Charity Parkerson
Editor: Hercules Editing and Consultants
ISBN: 978-1-946099-52-5
All rights reserved.

INTRODUCTION

DILLION NEEDS A KEEPER. BECK NEEDS A PLACE
TO LIVE. THEY'RE THE PERFECT MATCH. IN
EVERY WAY.

Being famous isn't everything, especially for someone too sweet for his own good like Dillion. Everyone takes advantage of Dillion. He doesn't know how to say no, even to save himself. Dillion has been quietly in love with someone who destroys him for way too long. When he meets a homeless waiter, Dillion does what he always does—comes to the rescue. Thankfully, his new friend has something Dillion desperately needs—courage to stick up for what's right.

Beck is having a hell of a day. He's stuck covering for a lazy co-worker while simultaneously getting evicted from his apartment. Luckily, his first customer of the day is Dillion Taylor, a famous child actor who is known all over the world. When Beck overhears Dillion's date being rude, he does what Dillion doesn't have the courage to do—he puts the man in his place. It's a moment that seals his fate as Dillion's next rescue mission.

While Dillion might not be brave enough to stand up for himself, he's an unmovable force when it comes to taking over Beck's life. It's Beck's bad luck that he also gets his heart stolen by the tiny angel, because Dillion is in love with a total dick. If Beck can't find a way to pry Dillion from his unhealthy obsession with someone nowhere near good enough to own him, he could lose his chance forever. That's one loss Beck can't survive.

ONE

DILLION STARED at the top of Kenneth's head and fumed. The man had perfect locks. That had nothing to do with Dillion's mood. Only one person ever enraged Dillion to the edge of murder—Mason Jacobs. They had been off and on for over a year. It had been the most hellish year of his life, but Dillion couldn't let go. He didn't know how. No one knew him like Mason. The fucker.

"Do you think Karma is real?"

Kenneth didn't even glance up from his phone. "Yes."

A loud snort came from over his head before a glass of water appeared in front. "No."

Dillion's gaze landed on the waiter. He looked as

aggravated as Dillion felt. He needed to talk to someone likeminded. "Right? I mean, if Karma is real, I'd love to know why so many shitty people end up with all the luck while I'm stuck here with this guy," Dillion said, motioning Kenneth's way.

Kenneth flashed him a disgruntled look. "Hey."

Dillion rolled his eyes. "Go back to playing your game."

The waiter nodded. "I hear ya. The girl who usually works this section called out every day last week, claiming she had the flu. In truth, she was in Vegas, partying with her friends while I was stuck covering her shift and mine. She was supposed to be back today, but when she came in, she quit. Turns out, while in Vegas, she met this woman who offered to pay her rent for three months if she moved to Vegas to waitress there. Plus, the woman is paying her twenty-two dollars an hour plus tips."

"Bitch."

The guy kept nodding. "Meanwhile, I woke up to an eviction notice because my rent check bounced because my ex cleaned out my checking account. But I can't even deal with that right now, because I'm covering the bitch's shift, and I need the money because now I'm homeless. Karma does *not* exist, and I'll fight any fucker who says otherwise."

"You're being rude," Kenneth said, sounding pious and annoyed. "You're working for us right now. Don't say 'fuck.'"

"Go back to your game," Dillion growled at Kenneth through his teeth. He pushed the empty chair at the table out with his foot. "Sit. What's your name?"

The guy looked around. "Beck. I better not. I can't lose my job."

Dillion flashed him a smile. "You're with me. You won't lose your job."

Beck nodded and sat. His sweet brown eyes focused on Dillion. "How is Karma fucking you?"

"It's stupid." It truly felt that way under Beck's intense stare, and in light of the guy's terrible morning. "My ex bought a new house with a guy he met at work. I shouldn't care." Dillion shrugged. "Except I didn't know he was once again my ex until I found out about the house... and the guy."

"Ouch. Yeah, there's no way Karma is real if that happened *and* you're with this guy," Beck said, motioning over his shoulder at Kenneth.

"Hey."

"Go back to playing your game," Dillion and Beck growled at the same time. They flashed each other a smile.

Beck's shoulders relaxed. They were nice shoulders. Wide but not obnoxiously so. He had great eyes too. They flashed with his every emotion. Wickedness poured from his smile. "You should slash his tires."

Dillion nodded. He liked this plan, but it wouldn't work. "I would, but I've already been arrested once for starting a fight at his work and keying his truck."

"Why did you start a fight at his work?"

Pain slashed through Dillion's heart. "He's the manager of a popular nightclub. I went there to see him one night and caught some guy giving him a hand job in the bathroom."

Beck curled his nose. "Ugh. Why do you even want this guy?"

"I don't," Dillion said without thought before the truth crowded his tongue. "I just don't... not want him." A wave of exhaustion washed over Dillion. He had never been more tired of being tired. "It's not that I'm weak." Dillion couldn't hold back those words. He wasn't weak. That wasn't why he couldn't let Mason go. He had shown Mason his heart and Mason had used it against Dillion at every turn. "Maybe I am." Dillion met Beck's stare again. He looked nice—like he didn't deserve the bad luck or being stuck listening to Dillion's problems. "Bring me the check, please. There's no hope for me, but I can help you."

Beck pulled a yellow slip of paper from his apron and handed it to Dillion. "I always keep the checks at the ready, in case people need to leave in a hurry."

Dillion nodded as he pulled out his wallet. "I think I'll be Karma today, since that bitch obviously isn't working. You deserve something good to happen to you." Dillion handed him a black credit card that was completely blank. "I'll take care of you."

Beck accepted the card. "You listened to me rant. That means more than you know." He stood and disappeared.

Dillion went back to staring at Kenneth's head. This was the last time he would choose a guy from a dating site. He obviously had terrible taste. He was about ninety percent sure Kenneth was straight. Either way, the guy wasn't really interested in Dillion. Dillion wasn't surprised. Men always found him too feminine or baby-faced. They didn't want someone like him. Someone with quirks. No one fit with Dillion. He was doomed to be alone. Love alone. His chest hurt.

"Here you go," Beck said, setting the card, receipt, and an ink pen in front of Dillion.

"Thanks," Dillion muttered as he filled in the blanks and signed the receipt. He handed it back to Beck. "There. Karma might not exist, but fairy godmothers do. Go take care of your rent."

Beck looked down at the receipt and back up at Dillion. "You can't give me a five-thousand-dollar tip."

"I can. I did. Go take care of things."

"Since we're not eating, can we go fuck now?"

Dillion's gaze hit the table at Kenneth's question. His eyes burned. He was so tired of living like this. It was like he was doomed to be used by everyone. Never loved.

"What the fuck?" Kenneth jumped to his feet. Dillion's chin shot up. Kenneth was soaking wet while Beck looked entirely too innocent holding an empty pitcher. Dillion didn't even know where the pitcher had come from.

"Oops. My hand slipped."

Dillion stared at Beck in shock. No one ever stuck up for him. Dillion stood. "What time do you get off?"

"I imagine I'm about to be fired, actually." Beck didn't sound worried. Just tired.

"Fuck this place. They make you work too much anyhow. Let's go."

Beck's eyebrows rose. He looked at Kenneth, who was still trying to wipe water from his lap with a single cloth napkin and back at Dillion.

Dillion flashed him a smile. It was the first genuine one he had managed in a long time. "Come on. I swear I'll make sure you're okay."

With an absent-looking nod, Beck took off his apron and tossed it onto the table. He walked with Dillion to the door. Dillion passed a bill to the guy working the door as they passed to cover his meal since Beck still held his check. He would make sure Beck got that five grand and more. Dillion didn't have many good people in his life. Today, he planned to rescue this one. A good mark in Karma's books, just in case. Maybe, someday, someone would save him too. All he had was hope.

BECK FOLLOWED ON DILLION'S HEELS IN A STATE of shock. He had never been anything but professional at work. Not that he was some straight-laced hard worker or something. He just liked having a roof over his head and wasn't particularly good at anything else. Something about losing his apartment had snapped his brain. Then that douche had treated Dillion like a whore. Everything about Dillion screamed sweet. He practically dripped sugar. Beck wanted to keep him safe. He wanted to fuck up that guy for daring to talk about soiling someone like Dillion. He was being ridiculous, no doubt. Beck couldn't help it. Life had sucked a lot lately. A moment of Dillion's attention had felt closer to friendship than he had experienced in a long while. Damn. He did a lot of stupid things.

Outside, Dillion headed for a black and white Bugatti Veyron. Beck had never seen one anywhere except in pictures online. It was the most badass car he had ever set eyes on. He was so enthralled; he didn't realize Dillion was on the phone until he handed it Beck's way.

"Tell the nice man your address."

Beck accepted the phone. "Why?"

"Because I asked you to," Dillion said, looking even younger in the daylight.

Beck shrugged, pressed the phone to his ear, and rattled off his address before handing the phone back. The sweet smile Dillion graced him with made Beck glad he had given in.

Dillion motioned to the passenger side of the multimillion-dollar car. "Get in."

Beck carefully opened the door and slid inside, hoping he didn't get anything dirty or accidentally scratch the paint. He couldn't afford to breathe the car's air. Dillion slid behind the wheel. Beck openly watched his every move. He was so damn beautiful. Beck was in awe. He had seen the movies Dillion had starred in as a child. Beck felt a bit perverted even looking at Dillion. In truth, Beck wasn't one hundred percent certain Dillion was over eighteen, but he clearly remembered the guy being a little kid and wowing the world. Beck shouldn't be sexualizing him. He couldn't stop. The guy had lips that looked delicious. A smattering of freckles painted his cheeks and nose. Eyeliner made his gorgeous light green eyes pop. Beck's gaze moved lower. Dillion had beautiful hands. There was a thin gold band on his middle finger and another on his thumb. Beck fought the urge to touch them. Dillion looked soft. He smelled good too—like candy.

"Your stuff will be here in the next few hours."

Beck blinked. He didn't remember a second of the drive, but they were pulling into a huge garage. Several expensive cars filled the space. Dillion parked between two. "Do you have a car I need to have picked up?"

Beck shook his head. "I usually ride the bus. Where are we?"

"My place," Dillion said, opening his door. "I have plenty of room. After I take you on a quick tour, you can tell me which room you want so I can tell the movers where to put your stuff." Dillion jumped from the car like he hadn't dropped a bomb on Beck's life.

Beck scrambled after him. "What do you mean?"

Dillion glanced over his shoulder. "I've decided to rescue you."

"Rescue me," Beck repeated. Even he heard the disbelief in his voice.

"Yep. You need some good luck. I've decided to give it to you. Come check out the house."

Beck knew there was some argument he should make. But he had lost his apartment, walked out on his job, and he was here. He found himself matching Dillion's steps and taking everything in. The pool shimmered to his left as they walked from the garage to the house. The house was unbelievable. While the huge mansion was made of stone, a majority of the house looked to be glass. Window after window—no doubt—looked out over an amazing view of the surrounding forest. There were no neighbors. Beck was beyond curious how much land Dillion owned. The place was stunning and easily worth millions. Still, Beck watched Dillion instead. Nothing else in his immediate sight held a candle to Dillion's beauty. Why didn't Dillion have a bodyguard? He shouldn't be out walking around, picking up strangers, and bringing them home alone. Anything could happen to him. Surely Dillion had stalkers and crazed fans around every corner. Why was no one caring for him? Protecting him? Who was this stupid mother fucker who'd moved in with another man? Whoever he was, he should be here, taking care of this irresistible man. Outrage owned Beck on Dillion's behalf.

"I could be a serial killer, you know?" The words burst from Beck with no input from his brain. He couldn't help it. Dillion was sweet. Too sweet. People like him ended up dead in ditches.

Dillion flashed Beck a smile as he opened the door for him. "Are you a serial killer?"

"No." After all, he had to be honest. "But I could've been. You don't know me. You shouldn't invite someone you don't know into your house."

Dillion blinked, as if the idea of anyone being a stranger eluded him. "Then tell me about yourself."

Beck cast a quick look around. They were inside the kitchen. It was a huge open space with quartz and steel. There was a nook in the corner. Beck moved to it and sat. He waited until Dillion sat too to start. "Okay. Well, I was a handful growing up and my parents finally got fed up and put me out at fifteen. The older lady who lived across the street took me in. She was poor, though, so I got out of her hair the moment I turned eighteen. Since then, I've spent the last ten years struggling to keep my head above water." He shrugged. "I guess that's it. Oh, my full name is Beckett Lee Jackson. My birthday is September fourteenth. What about you?"

Dillion shrugged. "You can Google me. Everyone knows everything about me."

"I don't," Beck admitted. "Obviously, I've seen your movies, but I don't know you."

For a moment, Dillion pressed his lips together and stared into space, as if trying to think of something to say. "Um. Well, I'm eighteen."

"Seriously?" Beck didn't mean to sound so disbelieving, but he felt like a huge perv.

A small chuckle escaped Dillion, sounding adorable. "Yep. Don't tell anyone because I literally just turned eighteen not that long ago. I hang out in a lot of clubs and everyone knows I'm not old enough to be there, but I'm famous." He shrugged as if that said everything, and really, it did. "If it makes you feel better, I feel like I'm eighty. I've been working since I was nine. My mom was very cutthroat. Even though she was a single mother, she spent her free time pushing me to be who I am. She didn't care what it cost me as long as I got the role. When I was fourteen, I realized she was stealing from me, so I hired a shark for a lawyer and won my freedom. I've been alone since then. About a year ago, I reconnected with my dad. He's chief of staff at All Saints Medical. Still, if I'm not hanging at Club Incubus, where my ex can torture me, I'm alone. I need a keeper. Someone to tell me no and make me go home when Mason settles for me."

"What do you mean?"

"My ex, Mason, when he can't find anyone else, he comes running. I always say yes. He always breaks me. I need help. So stay with me. Let me pay you to be my good sense."

"Don't you have friends for that?" Beck didn't mean to sound so harsh. He was more surprised than anything.

Dillion rubbed his arm and looked away. "Not really, no. People don't take to me very often. They find me strange."

"Are you strange?"

Dillion still didn't look his way. "Yes. I... Yes."

Beck's heart squeezed. No one should feel the way Dillion looked—like he didn't belong. And this Mason guy, fuck him. That was some bullshit. Beck didn't know Dillion, but from what he had seen, Dillion was amazing. He didn't deserve to feel alone and like he had been chosen last. "Okay." Dillion's gaze slid his way. It was filled with hope. "But," Beck added. "I don't want your money. You're letting me stay here. That's enough."

Dillion shook his head. "That's not enough. It's expensive to go out like I do, and—if you're tired from work—you won't want to close the place down."

"I don't want you to think we're friends because you're paying me, and I think that'll eventually happen if you're paying me."

The sweetest smile Beck had ever seen touched Dillion's lips. "I like you. Don't worry over my feelings. No one else does."

"I'm not like anyone else." Maybe Dillion had given up, but Beck hadn't.

Dillion's smile grew. His dimples deepened. Beck had to concentrate on controlling his breathing. He had never been so instantly struck by anyone. "Tell me what all you need. What do you like eat and drink? All of that. I'll get groceries delivered and we can watch movies tonight."

"Sounds great. Happy late birthday, by the way. I hope at least one person offered you the world."

Dillion pushed a dark curl behind his ear. A blush touched his cheeks as his eyes skirted away. "Maybe you're a late birthday present to myself."

Beck couldn't look away. He wasn't sure he cared what they did from here on out. He just wanted to know more about this person who'd taken over his life. Beck knew he should care or argue. He didn't. For years, he had been trapped in stasis with no hope of change. Now, no matter what happened, everything would be different afterward. He was excited for the first time in forever. Even if Dillion turned out to be psychotic, at least Beck wasn't still trapped waiting tables. That was something.

POOR BECK. HE LOOKED LIKE HE HAD BEEN HIT by a fast-moving train. Dillion bit back a laugh every time he looked the guy's way. Dillion had chosen the bedroom next door to his for Beck. It wasn't the biggest spare room, but it had the best bathroom. Plus, Dillion liked the idea of having someone right next door. It kind of felt like a friend had come to stay. Dillion's childhood hadn't been normal. He didn't have sleepovers or play dates. Dillion had a job. He had gone to work every day. From the sound of things, Beck's life had been the same but without the privilege of money. That was one thing Dillion could change.

"You know, I don't think this tub has ever been used."

Beck turned away from putting his clothes in the dresser and focused on Dillion at Dillion's observation. "I should try it out then, don't you think? That way, you'll feel like you've gotten your money's worth." He moved to join Dillion, sitting on the edge of the huge bathtub that took up one corner of his new bedroom. They both stared down at the jacuzzi tub. Beck chuckled. "Or not, since I'm not even sure how you work this thing. It's digital. I've never seen that."

Dillion shrugged. "We can figure it out." He pushed some buttons. Water began filling the tub. "Oh," Dillion said as realization hit. "It's pretty much like my shower." He pointed at a blue button. "This is the power button." He moved to a few up and down arrows. "This controls your water temperature, and these are your jet controls. You know, how powerful you want your jets and whatnot."

Beck nodded while switching between feeling of the water and playing with the buttons. He really was beautiful. Dillion couldn't stop staring at his long lashes. If Dillion did his makeup...

Sweet brown eyes flashed his way. "I wonder what would happen if we put bubbles in here."

An odd burst of excitement hit Dillion. "Hold that thought." He raced from the room and into his. Dillion found some bubble bath and headed back to Beck's room. He caught Beck stripping. "Oh, sorry."

Beck flashed him a smile. "Cool. You found some bubble bath."

Dillion crossed the room, moving slow in case Beck wanted him to leave. Beck kept peeling off clothing as if he didn't care Dillion was there, so Dillion didn't leave. Beck had a great body. It was sleek. He was tall. His muscles were well-defined. He wasn't a hulking beauty like Mason. Instead, Beck was like a swimmer—built for speed. Dillion drew a breath through his nose and poured the bubble bath into the tub. The jets immediately turned a small amount into a hill of bubbles.

Beck laughed and climbed in. "If this keeps growing, it'll swallow me." He didn't sound concerned. The humor tinting his words sounded like he was having a great time.

Dillion sat on the step near his head. "If it swallows you, I'll wash your hair. It's a passion," he said, flashing Beck a shy smile as he made the confession. "I like to play with people's hair."

Beck winked and disappeared beneath the water. He came up swiping his long bangs from his face. Dillion's cheeks ached from smiling. Beck was like a big kid. He made Dillion feel young. "I didn't think this through," Beck said, flashing him an apologetic smile. "There's no shampoo, towels, or anything in here."

Dillion glanced around. Beck was right. "Damn. Hold on." Dillion headed back to his bedroom. He grabbed everything he could think of that Beck might need before rejoining him. Beck had his head leaned back, relaxing on the edge of the tub. Dillion sat on the step beside him and stole his chance to eye Beck's body. He didn't want to notice how sexy Beck was, but the man was on full display. Dillion had a sudden desire to touch him. Beck's eyes opened. He stared at Dillion in silence. Heat grew between them, stirring butterflies in Dillion's stomach. He wasn't prepared to be attracted to anyone. Beck wouldn't want Dillion if he knew him.

Dillion grabbed the shampoo and squirted it in his hand to busy his mind. Some things were better left alone—like him. Dillion lost himself in scrubbing Beck's hair and scalp. He scratched, doing his best to bring Beck peace. Dillion had always liked washing other people's hair, massaging their heads, and mothering them. It made him feel human. He felt like he gave a piece of himself.

"Mason hates when I do this," he admitted without thought. "He says it's something only girls do, and he's gay for a reason." The words left a bitter taste in Dillion's mouth. Mason liked pointing out the things Dillion did that were too feminine. It wasn't as if Dillion didn't recognize all those things on his own. He didn't want to be a girl. Dillion just liked a lot of the same things as women.

With his eyes closed, Beck hummed. "Yeah. Fuck that guy. This is awesome. No one does things like this for me."

A smile tugged at Dillion's lips. "Good." He liked the idea of being someone Beck didn't already have. Dillion didn't know what they were. Friends, he supposed. Whatever they were, Dillion wanted more. He needed to be himself with someone. The constant hiding was suffocating.

"Okay. Rinse," Dillion said, forcing himself to

stop scrubbing. He dipped his hands in the water, washing away the shampoo as Beck disappeared beneath the water. When he resurfaced, Dillion started the whole process over again with conditioner. "You have great hair. It's so thick. I'm jealous."

A smile touched Beck's lips. He kept his eyes closed. "Considering how perfect your hair is, I definitely take that as a compliment."

Against his will, Dillion's gaze slid down Beck's body again. There was a smattering of dark hair on Beck's chest. Dillion tried focusing on it to keep his gaze from dropping lower. He didn't succeed. Despite his best efforts, Dillion found himself staring directly at Beck's cock. He swallowed. Even that part of him was nice.

"You have beautiful eyes. I noticed earlier you're wearing eyeliner. It really works for you."

Dillion's gaze shot to Beck's. He fought a blush at getting caught staring at the man's dick. "Um. Yeah. I guess I got used to it on the set and it eventually became a habit."

"You don't have to explain," Beck said, warming Dillion's heart. "It's your life. You're allowed to like whatever you want."

Dillion couldn't look away from Beck. No one ever made him feel normal.

"Is it time to rinse again?"

At Beck's question, Dillion forced himself back on track. "Yeah." He washed his hands in the water again as Beck rinsed the conditioner from his hair. Dillion fought the hope rising in his chest. It was odd how little he had thought about Mason all day. Usually, Dillion obsessed over every bit of drama happening between them. Today, he hadn't cared that much. Maybe he was finally breaking free. Dillion wanted that. He craved a different life. Maybe meeting Beck was the break he needed. It was possible Dillion wasn't a complete loss.

―――

BECK HAD NEVER BEEN MADE TO FEEL SO special. He wouldn't have thought being bathed as a grown man would be so sexy. It was the way Dillion was completely focused on him. When he had started stripping, Beck half expected Dillion would stop him or run away. The rest of Beck had hoped Dillion would join him. It had been a long shot, but still. Beck knew himself well enough to know he would regret it for the rest of his life if he didn't try.

He had learned a lot in the process. The biggest revelation for him was that Dillion was a nurturer.

This whole idea of bringing Beck to live with him wasn't some form of insanity. It was Dillion reaching for a lifeline. If anyone understood that, it was Beck. The thing was, Beck needed a lifeline too. His life was a complete mess. He had no one. His ex had left him months ago. Beck had forgotten the guy had access to his checking account until he had wiped Beck out and bragged about it. As if cheating on Beck and telling everyone how boring he was hadn't been enough. Fighting every day to survive didn't feel the least bit boring to Beck. It felt exhausting.

Dillion's eyes were really beautiful. Beck fought the urge to tell Dillion again how much he liked them. Instead, they sat in silence while Dillion continued washing Beck, as if he couldn't help himself—like he needed human contact. Dillion stared down at his hand as he trailed his fingers through the bubbles. Beck linked his fingers through Dillion's, stopping the motion.

Dillion's eyes shot to Beck's. "Sorry. I guess I spaced out."

"You don't have to apologize."

A shy smile touched Dillion's lips as he toyed

with Beck's fingers. The sight punched Beck in the chest. Dillion was beautiful and painfully lonely. That last one was something Beck could recognize from a mile away. It was what he saw each time he looked in the mirror. Even as Beck had unpacked his stuff, he had still been somewhat unsure if he should stay. Now he knew. He would stay for as long as Dillion needed him because—really—Beck needed Dillion more.

TWO

SINCE GROWING up and realizing he could choose his own career now, instead of doing what his mom had chosen for him, Dillion realized he still loved acting. He hadn't taken on any big roles in about a year, but Dillion still didn't rest. While most people hated doing interviews and going on talk shows, Dillion adored it. He had one woman in particular he always accepted invitations from— Coral Jones. Coral's show was fun and never deep. She didn't deal in gossip or hard-hitting topics. They just talked about life and fun events. Charities they both supported. Her shows were always a hit.

He made it halfway through the show, making cookies on live TV, before Coral asked him any personal questions. "I noticed you have a really hot guy with you today." The audience cheered, making Dillion realize someone had flashed a camera on a blushing Beck backstage.

Dillion glanced behind him at the huge screen on stage. A smile tugged at the corners of his mouth at the sight of Beck's face filling the space. He loved him already. "Yep. That's Beck. He's my guardian angel. I take him everywhere."

"Your guardian angel?" Coral asked as she poured some walnuts in a bowl.

Dillion nodded. "In this business, as I'm sure you know and have dealt with many times, we meet a lot of people who are out for themselves. I mean, really, it's like that for everyone. No matter who you are. Sometimes, I don't think people even realize they're doing it until it's too late and everyone is left disillusioned. It's hard to make friends as an adult. No matter who you are. Anyhow, Beck is the real deal. He's my friend."

Coral nodded along. Her blonde curls bounced along with the motion. Her blue eyes swung his way. "How did you meet Beck?"

"He rescued me," Dillion answered, throwing as much storytelling voice behind the words as he could, as he kept putting spoonful-sized globs of cookie dough onto cookie sheets. "I was on this horrible date. Horrible," Dillion repeated, dragging out the word. "The guy was being pervy, and I really didn't feel safe at one point. And here came Beck to save the day. He poured a pitcher of water in the guy's lap and swept me away. We haven't been apart since. He's super amazing."

"Awww! I love that," Coral cooed. "I'm glad he was there and kept you safe. It's dangerous these days out there in the dating world."

"Lord, you're not lying." At Dillion's words, the audience laughed, making Dillion's smile grow. He always ended up telling too much on Coral's show without her trying. Coral kept up the banter while Dillion did his best to keep up his side. His mind was on Beck. It was dangerous out there in the dating world. God knew he hadn't done well in that area. But he had hit the jackpot in friendship by meeting Beck. In fact, by the time the show ended, Dillion couldn't wait to get back to him.

Beck looked happy and a bit relieved when it was over. Dillion rushed to his side. "Are you ready to get back home?"

Beck shrugged. "I'm pretty content with wherever we go, but this town is a bit... not for me, I guess." Dillion got it. L.A. wasn't for everyone. Beck didn't give him time to say as much. "You looked like you had fun, though. I love watching you charm everyone. That story about how we met made me look a lot better than I am, but that was cute."

Dillion blinked at the statement. "What do you mean? I told the story exactly as it happened. You swept in like an avenger."

Beck chuckled and brought their linked fingers to his mouth, kissing Dillion's hand and making him realize they had been holding hands without thought. It was odd. They always touched each other, and Dillion couldn't say which of them reached for the other first. They simply had this indestructible bond Dillion couldn't explain. Even if they were only friends, Dillion recognized he had met his other half. A partner in crime to the end.

555-4376: *This is Mom. I saw you on The Coral Show and got your number from Ms. Langley. I can't believe it's been thirteen years since I saw my son's face. May I call you sometime?*

Dipshit: *I saw you on The Coral Show. You*

looked amazing. It made me realize how much I miss you. We should catch up.

WORK: DO YOU THINK YOU COULD COVER SASHA'S *shift tonight? I know you don't officially work here any longer, but we could always count on you.*

DIPSHIT: IF YOU HAVEN'T RETURNED MY TEXT *because of the money I took, I'm sorry. I plan to repay every cent. My car was about to be repossessed and I didn't know what else to do. I miss you.*

555-4376: BECK, I KNOW I'VE MADE A LOT OF *mistakes, but I'm still your mom. Please call me.*

DIPSHIT: WHATEVER. DON'T TEXT ME BACK. I *guess you think you're too good for me now that you're hanging out with celebrities.*

DIPSHIT: *I DIDN'T MEAN THAT.*

EVERYONE BECK HAD EVER MET OR DATED CAME out of the woodwork after Coral flashed his image on her show. Beck ignored them all. He had Dillion now. Being with Dillion didn't hurt.

For the tenth time, Beck's head bobbed, jerking him awake. In the past few months of living with Dillion, they never sat still. He had thought he would be bored not working. Dillion kept them too busy. He shopped. Traveled. Gave interviews. Guest starred on sitcoms. Anything and everything all the time. Tonight was the first night they had stayed in, and the exhaustion was quickly catching up with him. Beck never would have believed that doing nothing other than following Dillion around would be harder work than working. Not that he was complaining. Following on Dillion's heels came with a very sexy view. He was so tempted to go to bed, but Dillion's touch was too enticing. That was another thing Beck hadn't expected—to fall under Dillion's spell. He didn't think he was star struck. Beck thought he was snared by the single-minded attention he received.

"How long is this movie?"

Dillion ran his fingers through Beck's hair, scratching his scalp and threatening to put Beck to sleep. "I don't know. Another hour, I guess. You should let me style your hair. It's so soft and thick."

Beck blinked, fighting to stay awake. "I don't care. You can do whatever you want, especially if you keep this up. I like your touch." Beck snapped his teeth together, nearly biting his tongue in his attempt at shutting the hell up. Dillion was openly in love with someone else. That someone else sounded like a horrible asshole, but that wasn't Beck's business. He knew he should stop leaning Dillion's way, hoping for more head scratches—like a needy dog. But fuck, Dillion made it hard. His touch was addictive. No one treated Beck like this—like he was special. That was how Dillion won him.

Dillion lifted the arm rest between their theater-type seats, turning the dual recliners of the theater room into a large loveseat. "Here." He patted his lap. "Put your head here. I don't care if you fall asleep. You've had a busy day."

Beck didn't need to be told twice. He turned sideways facing Dillion, curled into a ball, and settled his head on Dillion's lap. Dillion went back to running his fingers through Beck's hair. Beck bit back a happy sigh. He moved closer to Dillion's stomach. Dillion smelled good—like chocolate chip cookies. It was odd, because they hadn't eaten any cookies, and Coral's show had been weeks ago, but— somehow—Dillion still smelled that way. Goddamn, it was like coming home. He didn't know how to describe what being with Dillion was like.

"I'm pretty sure you've always been my best friend. We've just been waiting around to meet." Beck didn't know where the confession came from, but it was the truth. It was the closest description he could find to how he had been feeling since they had met.

Dillion's fingers froze in Beck's hair. Beck's eyes opened. He found Dillion staring into space and looking thoughtful. After a moment, he went back to stroking Beck's hair. "That's an oddly fitting description of how I feel about us. I hope you don't get sick of me. Mason says I make people tired because I'm a toucher."

Beck wished Mason would rot in hell, but he kept it to himself. He still hadn't met this guy. Dillion steered clear of any place Mason might be. Still, Beck knew it was only a matter of time before they ran into one another. Beck wished he could make Dillion see himself the way Beck saw him before Mason did any more damage. "I'm curious how many times you've stopped yourself from doing things that make you happy because Mason has told you people don't like things about you."

Dillion chuckled. "Several times a day."

Beck shrugged. "Sounds to me like that's why he says things like that. As long as you think no one else could like you for you, you'll keep going back to him. No matter how shitty he treats you."

Dillion didn't respond. Silence dragged on while Dillion played with Beck's hair, making Beck feel like shit for having said anything. He didn't doubt for a second that Dillion knew he was treated like shit by the person he had given his heart to without Beck pointing it out.

Beck broke. "Sorry."

"For what?" Dillion said the words quietly as if he either didn't want to disturb Beck's rest or his throat hurt. Either way, Beck felt worse.

He shrugged. "Giving my opinion. Forget I said anything. I'll stay out of your relationship with Mason."

"There's no relationship with Mason," Dillion

said. His voice stayed soft. "He doesn't want me anymore."

"One last thing, then." Because Beck did not know how to stay out of things. "He's a fucking idiot."

The way Dillion shook with laughter had Beck's eyes opening. He had to see Dillion's laughter. Dillion stared down at him, smiling. "You should see how outraged you look." He brushed his thumb down Beck's nose. "Your forehead is all wrinkled."

Beck forced his features smooth and smiled. "I guess I get a little too opinionated sometimes."

"Close your eyes, sweetie. You need some sleep."

Beck did as told.

Dillion stroked his nose and traced his cheek before going back to massaging his head. "You shouldn't worry so much about my feelings. I'm stronger than I look."

"It's not about strength," Beck said, burying his nose against Dillion's stomach again, searching for the cookie scent. "You deserve better." He inhaled deep. "Damn." Even Beck heard the tired slur to his voice. "Why do you smell so good?"

"I don't know."

Well, fuck. That meant his cookie scent was natural

and Beck was super fucked. It was one more irresistible thing about a man who already had countless attributes Beck enjoyed. He needed to watch himself or he would wake up in love. Beck worried he might already be there.

———

DILLION STOPPED TRYING TO WATCH THE MOVIE to stare at Beck instead. Watching him sleep was infinitely more interesting than anything else. He was peaceful. Plus, it gave Dillion the freedom to stare at Beck until his heart was content without Beck knowing. Every day, it got a little harder to see him as only a friend. The problem was, Beck only saw Dillion as a friend and—despite spending every waking moment with Beck—Dillion was lonely. He missed being kissed. Dillion missed having someone hold him and stroke him. He was the overly touchy-feely person Mason accused him of being. Dillion liked being held. Going without affection had Dillion slowly withering away inside. This was why Mason always weaseled his way back into Dillion's life. Dillion didn't want to sleep alone.

His eyes burned. Dillion blinked against the tears. He knew he was weak even before he reached for his phone. His throat swelled as he found

Mason's number. Self-hatred filled his soul. Even as Dillion choked on the pain, he still sent Mason a text.

Dillion: *Hey.*

He quickly set his phone aside, vowing not to watch his message get delivered or search for the *read* to appear beneath his message. His phone buzzed. Dillion's eyes fell closed. He fought the urge to cry even as he opened his messages. No one knew how much it hurt.

Mason: *Wow. I didn't expect to hear from you again after the way things left off last time. What happened to you hating me?*

In a show of defiance against his heart, Dillion set his phone back on the end table—face down. Mason was right. Dillion did hate him. He went back to stroking Beck's hair. If his heart could take the beating of constantly being crushed by Mason, it could handle being alone. His phone buzzed again. Dillion ignored it. Beck had the perfect nose and eyebrows. It was an odd thing to fascinate Dillion, but he liked a flawless canvas. There were so many things he could do to Beck's features. He could completely change the man's looks with the right shading. Not that he wanted to change anything about Beck. Beck was a natural beauty. He didn't have to fight nature the way Dillion did. Dillion wasn't naturally soft or flawless. While he had gotten good at looking like he didn't wear a lot of makeup, he did. If only he could paint his insides too and make himself more appealing to others. Maybe then someone would love him. He blinked away tears at the dark thoughts. Depression was an ugly thing. He had tried counseling. It didn't work for him. Even when he paid someone to listen, Dillion still found himself pretending. He was an actor at heart. Dillion sugarcoated his thoughts any time he shared them. He didn't know how to reach for help. His phone buzzed again. Dillion's gaze slid its way.

"Are you okay?"

Dillion jumped at Beck's question. His gaze collided with the man's sweet brown eyes. "Yeah. Sorry. I thought you were sleeping."

"Just resting my eyes."

Dillion smiled. It didn't reach his heart. "You should go to bed. I've been running you ragged." His phone buzzed. Dillion's eyes fell closed. When they reopened, he found Beck watching him with knowing eyes.

Beck sat up. "Yeah. I'm pretty tired."

The urge to reach for Beck overcame Dillion. He

didn't move. Then Beck rolled to his feet and panic rose in Dillion's chest. "Beck."

Beck's gaze met his. "Are you sure you're okay?"

Dillion swallowed past the lump rising in his throat. If Beck left him alone, Dillion would answer Mason's texts. "Do you want to sleep with me tonight?" Dillion had no idea where the question came from. He knew exactly how he sounded, though—like he wanted Beck, because he did. Dillion didn't want Mason. Mason was the person he always fell back on, but he didn't want him.

"Your bed does look pretty awesome."

Dillion nodded. "It's like a cloud."

Beck's mouth lifted in one corner. "Okay."

With a chuckle and happiness restored, Dillion turned off the movie and came to his feet. He left his phone behind without looking back. Sometimes, in his darkest moments, Dillion did stupid things, but he wasn't dumb. Not really. It was also possible Beck was teaching him to save himself.

They headed down the hall. Beck looked over his shoulder. "I have to brush my teeth. Meet you in there?"

Dillion nodded. "Sounds good. I need to brush my teeth too and wash my face." Beck veered off to the left, heading inside his room, while Dillion moved on to his. He ran through his nightly routine before changing into a pair of workout shorts. He left his shirt off since he couldn't stand having a shirt twisting around him while he slept.

Beck appeared in the doorway, wearing the same basic outfit as Dillion. He pulled down the comforter on Dillion's bed. Dillion tried not to stare as Beck climbed beneath the covers, but he found himself hurrying to join him. With the lights off and a small space between them, Dillion was wide awake. He stared in Beck's direction, wishing they were closer. Beck's feet brushed Dillion's beneath the covers, making Dillion smile. Dillion moved too, intentionally brushing Beck's feet. A sexy chuckle rumbled from Beck's side of the bed. Dillion's cheeks hurt from smiling.

"Can I ask you something?"

"Of course." Dillion didn't need to think about it. He would answer anything Beck wanted to know, especially in the dark where secrets were shared.

"What made you decide to text Mason tonight?"

Dillion's mind went blank. Beck's question was the last one Dillion expected. He took a breath, wishing his chest didn't hurt. "I don't know."

"Do you miss him?"

Because Beck didn't sound judgmental, and it

was dark, Dillion chose to be honest. "No. I miss being held."

The bed shifted. Dillion's heart raced into his throat as he found Beck in his space. Beck's hand slid across Dillion's hip as he moved even closer. "You should've said something. I'm here. You're always spoiling me. I'm game to do the same in the only way I can." Beck's chest met Dillion's. Dillion found his face buried in the crook of Beck's neck. "Tell me what you need."

"I'm afraid of asking for too much. At what point will you think I've gone too far? When does it turn into me ruining things the way I always do?" Even Dillion heard the panic in his voice. If Beck got sick of him, Dillion would be alone again. He would end up beneath Mason's thumb again, begging for any scrap of attention. Each breath Dillion took came harder than the last until he thought he might hyperventilate.

Beck shifted again. This time, he buried his face against Dillion's throat and placed several loud kisses on Dillion's neck until he laughed and fought to get away. Beck held tighter, refusing to let him go. Somehow, Dillion managed to end up cradled against Beck with his back against Beck's chest. Beck went still, but he didn't let Dillion go.

"You're right," Beck said, as if nothing happened. "This bed is awesome. Can I sleep with you from now on?"

A surprised huff of laughter escaped Dillion. "Or I could buy you a bed just like this one."

"Nope." Beck's arms tightened around Dillion. "That's not the same. You're what makes this bed awesome. You smell good and I like to cuddle. Plus, you're warm and you fit perfectly in my arms. I think you need to let me sleep here."

Dillion shook his head at Beck's audacity. Yet he also couldn't stop smiling at Beck's audacity. His earlier unhappiness was gone. "In that case, you should sleep with me from now on. I'd hate for you to get cold."

"If you're going to beg."

A loud huff escaped Dillion. Being with Beck was invigorating. Dillion wouldn't text Mason again. He had been stupid. Maybe Beck didn't love him— not in a romantic way anyhow, but neither did Mason, and Beck didn't hurt him. A platonic love was better than the pain. He wouldn't torture himself any longer.

Beck's lips brushed Dillion's neck again. This time, it didn't feel quite as platonic. "Goodnight, sweet baby."

Dillion swallowed. "Goodnight, evil one."

Beck chuckled against Dillion's skin and Dillion knew he had made the right choice, asking Beck to sleep with him. Maybe they weren't a couple and never would be, but they were a pair. That was just as good in Dillion's book.

DILLION TIPTOED AROUND HIS PHONE ALL morning, eyeing it like a snake. He knew he had texts waiting, and he didn't want to see them. It was like Mason was there in the room, watching and finding him lacking. Beck broke before he did.

"Give me the phone. I'll get rid of all the evidence."

With a smile, Dillion tossed his phone Beck's way, barely missing knocking over the bowl of cereal he had perched on his knee. Beck easily typed in Dillion's passcode, proving they knew each other too well. He scrolled around and clicked a few things with one hand while still eating his cereal.

Dillion chewed his bottom lip. Beck didn't look upset. The texts must not have been horrible.

Beck glanced up and caught him watching.

"There's a message from someone named Summer. Do I need to get rid of that one too?"

"Awww, Summer. Gimme," he said, wiggling his fingers for the device. A smile tugged at Dillion's lips. He hadn't heard from Summer in weeks. As one of Incubus' bartenders, Dillion expected Summer to stop talking to him—like Mason got her in the breakup. It made him ridiculously happy to know she was still talking to him. The message was from this morning. That meant whatever texts Dillion received last night had been from Mason since they were now gone. In fact, every message between them had been deleted. It was for the best. He checked Summer's message.

Summer: *It's my birthday! Happy birthday to me. Come to Incubus tonight and celebrate with my new girlfriend, Autumn, and me. I'd love for you to meet her. Trace gave me the night off so I can drink with all my friends. Please say you'll come.*

A groan rose in Dillion's throat, but he didn't let it go. She was his friend. "How do you feel about hitting the club tonight? It's Summer's birthday."

Beck shrugged. "Whatever makes you happy. Who's Summer?"

"Oh." A burst of laughter sneaked out. Dillion covered his mouth. Beck's eyes swam with humor and Dillion couldn't get enough. "Sometimes it feels like we've been friends forever. I forget you don't know everything about my life. Summer is a bartender at Club Incubus. She's always been really nice to me. I don't really want to go to Incubus, but she asked."

"Will I finally get a look at this Mason guy?"

Dillion pulled a face. "Probably. He's the manager there. I don't want to stop living my life, though, you know?"

Beck nodded, looking thoughtful. "You should go. Let him see you don't need him. Plus, you need to prove to yourself that you can go, see him there, and be fine." Beck smiled. "Because you're so much stronger than you give yourself credit for. In fact, you're pretty fucking amazing. A superhero," Beck said, setting his bowl aside. He shifted onto his knees where they sat on the floor, leaned against the dual recliner, and tackled Dillion.

A loud cackle escaped Dillion as Beck tucked Dillion against his chest and dug his fingers into his ribs, stopping Dillion from getting away while he tickled him.

Dillion fought for his life until he couldn't breathe. Beck fell still and placed a loud kiss on Dillion's neck. He was one hundred percent a toucher—just like Dillion, and Dillion loved it. No one understood how lonely life was until they went untouched. Beck was everything Dillion needed. Dillion reached over his head and played with Beck's hair, because really, he lived for Beck's hair. "You called me a superhero," Dillion said with a chuckle.

"Yep. You saved me, so..."

Dillion couldn't stop smiling. "You really are the best person I know." It was easy to speak his mind with Beck's every breath brushing Dillion's throat and no one looking at him. "You could probably ask me for anything, and I'd make sure it was yours. I should buy you a car," Dillion said, getting excited at the idea of doing something special for Beck.

Beck kissed Dillion's neck again. This time, it was a light brushing of lips on skin that sent goosebumps rippling down his back. Dillion's eyes fell closed. If Beck dropped his arm a few inches from Dillion's waist, he would know exactly what he did to Dillion. "Do you know what I want?"

Wow. The way Beck's question felt against his neck had Dillion hoping whatever Beck wanted, it was physical. "What?" Dang. Even Dillion heard the lust in his voice. He bit his lip, trying to fight his desire.

"I want you to smile," Beck said, stroking

Dillion's stomach and making Dillion hurt with need. "and dance every slow song with me. Maybe hold my hand, so everyone thinks I'm good enough to have someone everyone else wants."

Dillion rolled onto his back. Seeing Beck's face was more important than getting busted with a hard on. "Do you not think you're good enough to have whoever you want?"

Beck's mouth lifted in one corner. He kept stroking Dillion's stomach. "In truth, I think I'm pretty ordinary. There's nothing about me that stands out in a crowd or anything." He shrugged. "I'm just me."

Dillion stared at Beck. He was beautiful. Inside and out. Maybe he didn't have any overly striking features, but he had the kindest eyes Dillion had ever seen. He knew they were truly a window to Beck's soul, because Beck had the best heart. A lump formed in Dillion's throat. If they had met at Incubus, Dillion probably wouldn't have picked Beck from the crowd. The day he had met Beck, Dillion had struck gold and hadn't realized it when it happened. Now he recognized that he had been shallow many times in his life. There was no one more beautiful in all the world than Beck.

"I'd choose you over absolutely anyone any day

of the week." The sincerity in Dillion's voice couldn't be missed. Beck set his chin on Dillion's chest. Dillion went back to playing with his hair. There was nothing left to say. Maybe they weren't a couple and maybe they never would be, but they were still each other's greatest loves, and if this was all they ever had, they would still be perfect. Dillion kissed Beck's forehead. They were amazing and enough.

THREE

CLUB INCUBUS WAS JUST A CLUB. It was a nice club, with lots of space and good music, but it was still just a club. To some extent, Beck had built the place in his head as a pretentious place that was full of people like Mason and nothing else.

Dillion had a lot of pretty friends. In fact, Beck was feeling downright plain next to the group Dillion introduced him to. Summer was amazing. She was funny and gorgeous. Her girlfriend was equally amazing. Even though Dillion had introduced him to a couple of his guy friends, Beck found himself sticking to Summer's side and trying not to feel inferior. After all, the huge bald guy and blond guy with laughing eyes were too much of everything for Beck's comfort.

Summer laughed about something he couldn't hear over the music. She leaned his way as if intent on retelling the story to Beck. The humor in her expression fell away. Her blue eyes flashed with annoyance. "Fuck. Here comes Mason."

Beck's head whipped around, following her line of sight. A large red-haired man with a cocky smile and huge bulging muscles moved in their direction. He was way hotter than Beck expected. That detail made Beck's heart sink. He didn't stand a chance against this guy. That was the only thought Beck had time to process before Mason was in his space. His eyes flashed with interest. He moved even closer. His mouth lifted in one corner in the most lecherous smile Beck had ever seen. The guy dripped sex and bad decisions—like he would wreck Beck's body and then level his life.

"I'm Mason," Mason said, eyeing Beck from head to toe. "We should find a dark corner and get to know each other, don't you think?"

Beck held up his hands—beer and all, showing he wasn't touching Mason. He didn't care if he looked like an idiot because Beck knew only one thing with absolute certainty—he couldn't let Dillion think for a second he was interested in what Mason had to offer. His gaze slid Dillion's way. Dillion's expression broke Beck. He kept his gaze carefully averted. Beck could feel the waves of pain rolling from him. He couldn't understand anyone treating Dillion the way this bulky asshole did. Dillion had a beautiful soul, one that deserved to be cherished. Beck set his beer aside, stepped around Mason, and moved Dillion's way. Dillion's gaze landed on him and didn't budge. No one looked at him the way Dillion did—like he was important. Beck had always been a lowlife piece of shit whose parents didn't even want him. Yet, for whatever reason, Dillion had taken him in like a stray and loved him, even if it was only platonic. It was the only love he had ever been given. Beck wouldn't stand aside and watch Dillion whither beneath someone's mistreatment. There was no way he would let Mason's flirting hurt Dillion.

He didn't know what Dillion saw in his expression, but Dillion didn't move. Even as Beck stood, hovering over Dillion, Dillion's chin turned upward, and his gorgeous gaze held Beck's. Without a word, Beck reached for Dillion. His hands slid across the man's hips. He towed him closer. Dillion let it happen. Everyone else disappeared. Beck lowered his chin, giving Dillion plenty of time to push him away. Dillion didn't move. Beck took his chance. He claimed Dillion's mouth. With his lips pressed to Dillion's, Beck felt Dillion's breath catch. Then, his lips parted beneath Beck's. Their tongues brushed. Dillion's hands slid up his chest. His arms encircled Beck's neck. He shuffled closer. Beck's heart didn't stand a chance. Dillion's kiss was every bit as sweet as the man. Beck wanted to sweep Dillion into his arms and walk away from this place.

The room spun. It took Beck a moment to realize he had been ripped away from Dillion like a doll. He caught sight of an enraged Mason a half second before his massive fist headed for Beck's face. Beck ducked. He wasn't quick enough to get completely out of the way. Mason's punch still grazed him. Dillion appeared, looking like an avenging angel as he leapt through the air and onto Mason's back. Screams and shouts assailed Beck's ears. Several people joined the melee, making it impossible to know what was happening. A blonde woman who worked the bar tried getting between Dillion and Mason. It was beyond obvious that Mason didn't know how to handle an attack from Dillion. He was visibly trying not to hurt Dillion while Dillion didn't hide the fact that he had every intention of hurting Mason. He looked enraged and beautiful. Even as hands tugged at Beck, dragging him from the bar,

Beck couldn't look away. People pushed and tugged, forcing the fight outside.

"Stop, baby. Calm down," Mason yelled to a Dillion who wasn't having it. "He shouldn't have been touching you. Fuck. Don't pull hair," Mason begged as he tried talking Dillion down.

A young dark-haired and light-eyed guy who was every bit as small as Dillion stepped from the club. It was like his presence alone was powerful enough to cast a calm over the crowd. Dillion leapt away from Mason, dodging the guy's beefy arms as he tried snagging Dillion around the waist. Beck got to Dillion first, pulling him back against his chest. Dillion deflated, molding against Beck's body. The way he shook had Beck's heart flip-flopping. He wanted to make Mason pay, but he equally wanted to cling to Dillion and keep him safe.

"What in the hell is wrong with you, Mason?" the new arrival said, sounding unnaturally calm. "I promoted you to manager to keep the club's best interest at heart, but now you're starting fights."

Before Mason had time to answer, the guy turned away and focused on Dillion. "I think you need a break from this place. Don't come back for a while."

Dillion's already small body seemed to get even smaller. He nodded. "I'm sorry, Trace."

Trace's shoulders fell. He swiped his hand over his eyes. "Don't be sorry. I saw everything. You were just sticking up for your friend, but damn, Dillion. Mason and you are just too volatile when you're in the same place. I know you two try to be civil, but fuck. This is my business we're talking about. I already risked everything by letting you come here before you were eighteen."

Dillion kept nodding. "I know. I'm sorry. I won't come back again."

"Goddamn it," Trace cursed, sounding even more pissed by Dillion's acquiescence. "That's not what I want."

Beck couldn't help but notice Mason wasn't apologizing or offering to stay away. The dick. Beck hated the guy a little more with each passing moment. He tightened his hold on Dillion. "Come on, sweetie. Let's go home. I'll let you pull my hair until you feel better."

Dillion stroked his chest. "I'm so sorry you were dragged into this. Are you okay?" He tried getting a better look at the side of Beck's head where Mason's punch landed while urging Beck toward the car. "I'll run you a bath when we get home and wash your hair. That always makes you feel better."

"Hold on. Wait one fucking minute," Mason yelled while attempting to chase them down. The huge bald guy Beck had met earlier kept Mason in check. "Does this guy live with you? What the fuck, Dillion? Does he even know the real you? Have you shown him?"

Beck didn't know what Mason was going on about, but he could feel the way Dillion got smaller with each question. He did the only thing he could think to do: he swept Dillion from his feet and headed for the car without looking back.

"Don't look back, sweetie," Beck said for Dillion's ears alone. "He likes it when you hurt." Beck would make it better.

———

HE LIKES IT WHEN YOU HURT. THOSE WORDS bounced from the walls of Dillion's brain—stuck on repeat like a mantra. The ring of truth to Beck's words cut Dillion to the bone. Several times he had wondered if Mason secretly hated him. That was the only thing that made sense. If Mason had ever told Dillion something he did or said hurt him, Dillion would move heaven and earth to stop. With Mason, Dillion always felt the need to hide his weaknesses because he knew Mason would use them to twist Dillion into knots. In one night, Beck had seen what Dillion turned a blind eye to for over a year—this wasn't love. It was hate. In the past few months, Beck had shown him what real love looked like. It didn't hurt.

Dillion drove home on autopilot. He had lost his usual hangout spot for good. That stung, but it was also oddly freeing. His shoulders felt lighter. Dillion never had to step foot in the same building as Mason again. The final tether had been cut. Dillion rubbed his chest. The image of Mason, smiling down at Beck with sexual intent, cut Dillion to the bone, but not because of Mason. The instant choking fear of losing Beck in that moment had nearly brought Dillion to his knees. He could survive a lot. In fact, he already had survived more than most, but losing Beck would kill him. Beck was the only thing keeping him breathing most days. He needed that link.

They sat in Dillion's car, parked inside the garage, and staring at nothing. Dillion leaned Beck's way and reached for his hand. Beck didn't hesitate linking fingers with him. Dillion brought Beck's hand to his lips. Mason had hit him. Dillion's throat swelled. He wished Mason dead in that moment. Beck had gotten hit because of Dillion. He couldn't breathe at the thought. Dillion was a plague on Beck's life. He gave Beck nothing while demanding everything.

"Dillion."

Dillion's eyes flew open. His gaze shot Beck's way. He sucked air, but no oxygen reached his brain. Mason had hit Beck. Seriously. He had watched it happen. His eyes filled with tears. Then, Beck was there. His mouth covered Dillion's in his darkest moment—exactly as he had done at the club, breathing fresh life into Dillion. Their tongues met and played. Beck gently held Dillion's face as he ravaged Dillion's heart. Loud breaths filled the car. Beck's kiss was amazing. It was sweet and hot with a huge helping of skill. Dillion surrendered to it. He covered Beck's hand on his cheek and held it there. Dillion couldn't let Beck get away. That first kiss at Incubus had left Dillion wondering if it had been for show. A fuck you to Mason. This kiss was one hundred percent about Dillion. He felt Beck's hunger all the way to his soul.

"We should go inside." Beck's lips brushed Dillion's with every word.

Dillion nodded and slipped from Beck's hold.

He waited for Beck. Without thinking about it, he reached for Beck's hand. They clung to each other in some way all the way to the bedroom they now shared. Side by side, they stripped to their boxer briefs. As one, they climbed into bed, like they had been doing so for years. Dillion curled into Beck's arms. He clung to the man's chest while Beck pet him, keeping him safe and making him feel loved.

Dillion swallowed past the lump in his throat that grew larger by the second. "I owe you so many apologies."

Beck shifted forward, forcing Dillion onto his back. He kept moving until his body covered Dillion's. Dillion blanked. He forgot to breathe, especially when he realized how hard Beck was... everywhere. Beck's lips skimmed Dillion's throat. A moan escaped Dillion before he could stop it.

"No more thinking," Beck warned as he moved lower, kissing Dillion's shoulder. Dillion's hips lifted. He moved restlessly against Beck. Dillion didn't realize Beck held his wrists until Beck's lips closed around Dillion's nipple. His inability to touch Beck in return was the most freeing moment of Dillion's life. He didn't have to make any decisions. Dillion was at Beck's mercy. Under his control.

Beck urged Dillion's hands above his head. "Hold on to the headboard. If you let go, I'll stop."

Dillion wrapped his fingers around the wood and held tight. The last thing he wanted was for Beck to stop touching him. Maybe he would regret this later, but he doubted it. No one knew exactly what he needed and gave it to him the way Beck did. This was no different.

"Good boy," Beck growled, going back to kissing and nipping at Dillion's chest. Dillion's heels dug into the mattress, but he didn't let go of the headboard. He sucked in a sharp breath as Beck's tongue traced his sternum and moved lower, licking down the center of Dillion's chest. He moved lower. Dillion whimpered as Beck kissed his stomach. His cock strained to get Beck's attention. When Beck's fingers curled around the waistband of Dillion's shorts, Dillion's hips automatically lifted. He wanted everything Beck did. "I have all the attention you need. No more Mason."

"Okay." Even to Dillion's ears, he sounded desperate.

"You don't get to feel lonely, neglected, and mistreated on my watch. Understood?"

"I understand." Dillion would have agreed to anything. He had tried hard not to be attracted to

Beck. Dillion didn't want to ruin their friendship. He was too turned on to think about any of that now. Then Dillion's cock was in Beck's mouth. Dillion couldn't focus on anything else. Beck caressed him every place he could reach. Dillion knew he was about to come entirely too fast. It had been too long since anyone touched him like this, and goddamn, Beck had talent. He put his fucking heart into blowing Dillion.

"Beck."

The pleading in his voice obviously broke through to Beck. Beck's gaze flipped upward, holding Dillion's stare as he sucked. Dillion almost lost it right then, but he wanted more.

"I'm empty. I want you inside me."

Beck swiped his face on Dillion's stomach. "I don't have any condoms or anything."

Fuck. "I don't either," Dillion admitted, hearing the disappointment in his voice and incapable of hiding it. He wanted Beck.

Beck held his stare, looking confused. Dillion felt as bare as he was. "You don't even have lube?"

Dillion shook his head.

The line between Beck's eyes deepened. "I can't believe I'm about to ask this. Didn't Mason ever stay here?"

Without his permission, Dillion's gaze slid away. "Mason and I never actually had sex. I mean, I haven't been eighteen that long and Mason likes having his dick sucked..." Jesus. He felt like an idiot and he did not want to be having this discussion right now. The mood was starting to wither away. At least for him. When he looked back Beck's way, Beck stared at him with a hunger Dillion had never seen. His mouth went dry.

"Are you saying you're a virgin?"

Dillion couldn't look directly at Beck. "Well, I mean, I've done other things. So I guess it depends on what you consider to be the definition of sex. That's a pretty deep question."

Beck climbed from the bed. Dillion's heart dropped. No one ever wanted him. At least Mason had seen the real him before deciding he wasn't interested in sex with Dillion. He had always claimed it was their huge age difference, and he wasn't about fucking a kid. Not that Dillion's age had stopped Mason from taking him home to get blown. Every second that passed, the more Dillion's heart sank. He wished he was normal. Dillion wished he was someone who made a boyfriend proud. Instead, he was this...

Beck reappeared at the edge of the bed holding

the coconut oil Dillion kept in his bathroom for skincare. He stood over Dillion, looking serious. "I've never slept with anyone without a condom and you've never been with anyone at all. You can stop things now, and I can finish what I started earlier. Or you can admit you're mine and I can make love to you without the condom. You decide. But if you say you're mine, you can't take it back. I'm way too possessive to let you go. Plus, like I said, I'm not the type to go bareback."

Dillion swallowed. He was Beck's, but that wasn't enough. "Are you mine?" Mason had taught him the two things weren't synonymous.

Beck nodded. "I've belonged to you since you decided to keep me."

"Can I let go of this headboard and touch you now?"

Beck visibly fought a smile. "Yes."

Good. His arms were starting to hurt. "For the record, you completely own me. You have since you dumped a drink on my date."

"That wasn't a date," Beck said, climbing onto the bed. "A date takes you out. Makes you proud. That guy was a leech." Beck grabbed a pillow. "Lift your hips." Dillion did as Beck ordered while Beck kept talking and shoved the pillow beneath Dillion's hips. "If you'd been with me, I would've had my chest all puffed out, because damn. You're beautiful." He kissed Dillion's stomach and unscrewed the lid on the oil. "I would've done everything I can think to do to make you happy, because you're worth it to me."

A lump formed in Dillion's throat. He couldn't stop brushing his fingertips over every place he could reach on Beck's body. Dillion had never been this happy. No one made him feel special the way Beck did.

Beck's gaze moved over Dillion's nude body. "You really are completely perfect. How are you totally hairless? Like that's fascinating me. You're smooth and soft. It's sexy as fuck."

Dillion chuckled. "It's also so very vain of me. I had laser hair removal."

Beck shook his head as he scooped out some oil. "You can call it vain if you want. I just want to fucking lick you." He massaged Dillion's cock, coating it with oil before moving lower. Dillion moaned. Between Beck's earlier attentions and his slippery fingers, Dillion was so ready. He wasn't scared. The way Beck kept talking kept Dillion's nerves at bay. He recognized that was why Beck did it, but he still fell victim to Beck's charms. He spread his thighs at Beck's urging. Dillion couldn't hold a thought while Beck toyed with his balls and fingered his hole.

The hunger on Beck's face was almost Dillion's undoing. If anyone had ever wanted him more, Dillion hadn't noticed. It was intoxicating being desired. "Beck, I know you're being sweet, but I kind of want you too bad for this much kindness."

Beck stopped playing. His gaze met Dillion's. For a moment, he simply let Dillion see his hunger and Dillion realized he should be scared. Beck was barely holding himself in check. "I want to kiss you."

Dillion fought a whimper. It was such a simple statement. The words sucker-punched Dillion like Beck had whispered the dirtiest of scenes against his ear. "Please?"

Beck shifted onto his knees and pushed his shorts down his hips, stripping. Once he was nude and Dillion was panting. He slipped between Dillion's thighs and covered Dillion's body with his. When their skin met, Dillion sucked in a hiss. Every nerve he possessed was on high alert. Then Beck's lips brushed his. Dillion opened, touching his tongue to Beck's. They moved, tasting each other. It was heaven and hell. Dillion loved everything about Beck's touch, but he wanted more. He wanted Beck's thick cock pounding inside him. The fantasy he had secretly touched himself to in the shower was moments away from becoming reality and Dillion thought he might break. Even though no one had ever been inside him, Dillion wasn't stepping into the unknown. He had used those suction cup dildos that stuck to the shower wall. He knew what angles worked for him and how it felt.

Then, Beck's crown brushed his asshole. Dillion realized it wasn't at all the same. The intimacy was beyond anything he had ever experienced. He felt like they were becoming one. Their souls were touching. Beck was so gentle. He treated Dillion like glass. His dick pushed inside Dillion a tiny bit before quickly retreating. Beck's kiss turned wild like that hint of penetration had been amazing. Dillion's body reacted, matching the fire of Beck's kiss. Pre-cum soaked his stomach. A hungry sound escaped Beck as he thrust again. Dillion's cock twitched as Beck went a little deeper. He thought he might scream his frustration. Dillion was beyond Beck being gentle. He wanted to get fucked. His body craved. When Beck pushed deeper next, Dillion stole his chance. With his heels buried in the mattress, Dillion thrust upward, impaling himself. Beck gasped around Dillion's tongue. Dillion moaned. He hadn't been prepared at all for the fullness. The pressure. The pleasure. His dick twitched hard.

Beck snapped. With Dillion's thigh held tight in his grip, he pumped inside Dillion. His aim was fucking perfect. He hit the right spot with every thrust, massaging the button that had Dillion seeing stars. Cum exploded from Dillion's cock with almost no warning. There was no slow build. One second, he thought he was close and the next, he was soaking their skin with his juice.

"Goddamn, baby. You're so fucking hot and responsive. I'm not going to last. Your tight ass is sucking me dry. Fuck, Dillion." Beck threw his head back. The muscles in his neck strained as Beck rode Dillion's ass. Dillion gasped for air and enjoyed the show. Beck was so sexy. He stole Dillion's heart. Beck gasped as he came. He dropped his chin and held Dillion's stare as he filled Dillion's ass with cum. Dillion lost a piece of himself in that moment. No one else would ever be enough again. Beck was the one for him.

FOUR

THEY HAD LOCKED THEMSELVES AWAY, doing nothing more than cuddling on the couch for days. Beck couldn't think of a single thing he would rather be doing. He couldn't stop thinking about how they had gotten here. Beck realized they had been heading here since they met. No one could tell him they weren't meant to be. Beck felt it in his gut.

They toyed with each other's fingers, stole kisses, and did nothing more than savor each other's company. It was almost funny. For the most part, it was the same way they always spent their days, but now their feelings were out there. They didn't have to hold back, afraid of crossing a friendship line. That line had been obliterated, but they were still best friends. To Beck, they were perfect. He hoped

Mason stayed away. That was the only thing that could dampen Beck's happiness. He really hated that bastard.

"What are you thinking about? You look so intense right now."

The smile in Dillion's voice had Beck's heart singing. Damn. He was in love. Since he couldn't say that, Beck went with as close as he could get. He moved Dillion's hand to his lips. "That all these are yours," he answered, kissing Dillion's palm before taking his hand lower and holding Dillion's palm over his beating heart. "And every one of these beats are for you."

A flush rose on Dillion's cheeks. His lips parted. He looked engaged with every sense. Dillion slowly slid his hand lower, stroking Beck's chest and stomach. Beck's cock stirred. By the time Dillion massaged Beck's dick through his shorts, Beck was completely hard. "What about this? Is this mine too?"

Beck nodded. "You own the entire package. Any piece of me you want, it's yours."

"What if what I want is to keep you forever?" Dillion immediately bit his lip, as if he couldn't believe what he had said. He was so adorable. Beck wished he could spoil Dillion. Give him the world.

All he had to offer was himself. His actions and his words. "That was my plan." He toyed with Dillion's fingers. "Tell me what I can do to show you a hint of what you do for me every day. How can I baby you?"

Dillion stole a quick kiss before responding. "Do you remember that bubble bath you took your first day here?"

"Of course. I tried hard to tempt you to join me, but you seemed pretty immune to my charms." Beck couldn't hide the laughter in his voice. It became a full belly laugh as Dillion covered his face with both hands.

"Are you kidding me?" Dillion sounded horrified and entertained.

Beck couldn't stop laughing. Being with Dillion was always amazing. "Nope. You handled yourself with aplomb. It was like you have people strip in your presence every day."

Dillion dropped his hands. His eyes swam with humor. "I'm obviously not good at taking hints. It's a good thing that was about to be my suggestion. I missed out that day. You have no idea how badly I wanted to climb into that tub with you."

"Let's do it." They exchanged a smile Beck felt all the way to his soul before they scrambled to their feet. As they raced to the door, Beck swept Dillion off his feet and tossed him over his shoulder to peals of laughter. A loud crash came from the kitchen, freezing Beck's feet to the floor.

"What was that?" Dillion asked in a stage whisper.

Beck set Dillion on his feet and pushed him behind his back before heading to the kitchen. Dillion held his shoulders, staying glued to Beck's back.

"Don't call the police." The words were yelled in Beck's face, sending his heart racing into his throat, as a guy he had never seen before leapt from the kitchen into his path.

"Falcon!" Dillion pushed his way around Beck and launched himself in the guy's direction. Even though they were the same size, Falcon didn't flinch or get rocked on his feet as Dillion climbed him like a monkey and kissed all over the guy's face.

Falcon laughed as he hugged Dillion. It was a sexy sound. Jealousy owned Beck. It didn't help that the guy was unbelievably gorgeous. His dark hair was perfect, and his eyes were an eerie light gray.

"Hello, sweet baby."

A growl rose in Beck's throat as the guy used Beck's pet name for Dillion. He refused to let it fall. Beck had known what he was in for when he fell for

Dillion. The man was famous. Everyone wanted him.

The eerie gray eyes swung Beck's way as he hugged Dillion. "Who is the too sexy dude who's eyeing me as if he plans to kill me if I don't step back?"

At Falcon's question, Dillion slipped to the floor, but he held tight to Falcon's waist. He turned his smiling face Beck's way, looking happier than Beck had ever seen. "Falcon, this is my boyfriend, Beck." Beck was mollified by that. "Beck, this is my oldest friend, Falcon. We grew up together. He was my stuntman in every movie I've ever done."

Falcon moved closer, holding out his hand for Beck to shake. "It's nice to meet you, Beck. I'm sorry to burst in on you like this. Usually, when I'm in town, my entrance isn't quite so spectacular. I knocked over a fucking suitcase in the dark that was by the door."

Oops. They still hadn't unpacked from their recent trip to L.A.

"He has a key," Dillion said unnecessarily.

"I rarely use it," Falcon said, as if trying to comfort Beck. His gaze moved Dillion's way and his features softened. Until it happened, Beck didn't realize how much his name fit. Falcon looked fierce and dangerous. He might not be very big, but Beck got the impression people didn't fuck with him. "I've missed your face, babe. But I'm damn glad to see someone finally has you smiling."

Dillion's gaze slid Beck's way. He blushed, making Beck's stomach growl. Beck had never felt so possessive and hungry. Dillion was his. The blush was for him. "You'll like Beck. He's pretty amazing."

The jealous beast that Dillion had stirred inside Beck finally quieted at Dillion's claim. Falcon might be sinfully sexy, but Beck was who Dillion had chosen.

"I can't wait to get to know you," Falcon said, bringing Beck's gaze his way. "But you two should get back to whatever you were doing before I burst in. I was just dropping my stuff off before I'm off to do a shoot."

"You have a fight?"

Falcon nodded.

Beck looked between them. "A fight?"

Dillion flashed Beck a bright smile. "Falcon runs an online channel, posting videos of his street fights all over the world." He pulled a face. "It's pretty brutal. Do you want to go?"

Falcon made a dismissive motion before Beck

could answer. "Everyone knows your face. I don't want the police showing up at your door."

Dillion's face fell.

It was Beck's job to make him happy. "It's pretty cold out tonight. You could wear a thick coat and a scarf over the bottom half of your face. Plus, I could block you from prying eyes."

Falcon glanced between them. Dillion was back to looking hopeful. Beck could see Falcon folding. "You'd have to either ride with me or take a different car. The Bugatti draws too much attention."

"We can take the Cayenne. I only drive that one when it snows. No one will recognize it." Dillion practically bounced in place as Falcon nodded.

"All right. I'll text you the directions. Get dressed."

A loud squeal rent the air as Dillion raced down the hall. Beck flashed Falcon a smile before following at a slower pace. When he closed the bedroom door, Dillion looked his way and froze. His smile slipped away. "Is this okay with you? Really? I mean, we had a different night planned, and I just bowled over all that."

Beck hated the glimpses of insecurity Dillion occasionally showed. In these moments, he saw the way Dillion had been mistreated in the past. He saw how Dillion expected anger and retaliation. Beck closed the distance between them. "Will we be together tonight?"

Dillion's brow furrowed, as if Beck's question confused him. "Of course."

"Then I'm happy. Being with you is all I care about. The tub will still be waiting later." He shrugged. "I just want to be with you. Whatever you're doing, I want to be part of it."

Dillion blinked fast as if fighting tears. He nodded and looked away. "Okay. I didn't want you to be disappointed." Dillion's voice sounded strained. Beck couldn't take it. In a flash, Beck was in Dillion's space, forcing his chin up and claiming his mouth. It was a deep, hard kiss. Dillion kissed him back with every bit as much desperation as Beck felt.

He backed away before things went too far and Dillion missed his friend's fight. Beck swiped away the moisture from Dillion's bottom lip, enjoying Dillion's dazed expression. "Get dressed, sexy." They had a long night ahead of them. Beck wanted to get the show on the road. After all, the quicker this fight ended, the faster they would be in the tub. Beck desperately wanted that bath.

Beck was right about no one noticing him. Of course, Beck did an amazing job of blocking Dillion from anyone looking too closely at him. Plus, it was cold, and Dillion didn't want to leave the warmth of the scarf covering his face. Falcon's fight was every bit as brutal as Dillion recalled. Since Falcon was a small guy and famous for these illegal brawls, everyone always challenged him. Of course, they never took into account that Falcon was a martial arts master and had trained his entire life. He might be small-framed, but he was deadly, and the fight ended without a single blow landing Falcon's way.

Dillion and Beck clung to the edges of the crowd, waiting for it to disperse so they could spend more time with Falcon. The later it got, the colder it got, and the closer Dillion huddled to Beck. He shoved his hands inside Beck's coat, looking for a warmer place.

Beck jumped as Dillion's ice-cold fingers collided with his skin. "Shit, baby. Why didn't you tell me to get your gloves?"

"I didn't want you to leave me," Dillion answered honestly. He felt safe with Beck around. Beck pressed his lips to Dillion's forehead before snagging Falcon's attention.

"Falcon! Watch him," he yelled, motioning Dillion's way. "I have to run to the car."

Falcon nodded and moved closer. Beck waited until he ensured Dillion would be fine before jogging toward the SUV. The instant he was out of earshot, Falcon attacked. "Tell me everything."

A snort of laughter escaped Dillion. "What do you want to know?"

"Everything," Falcon said. His eyes swam with laughter. "Where did you meet? How long have you been together? It's obviously love, but does that mean he knows everything about you? Like, has he seen the real you yet?"

"Found them," Beck said, reappearing faster than expected.

Dillion prayed Beck hadn't heard. He hadn't exactly been hiding since Beck moved in, but he was starting to twitch on the inside from avoiding his usual release. Staring at Beck's face told him nothing. Beck kept his gaze locked on the task of putting Dillion's gloves on. When he finished, he dropped to one knee and tied Dillion's boot that had obviously come untied at some point. He glanced up and smiled. "We can't have you tripping over your shoestrings."

Dillion couldn't look away from Beck's upturned

face. If he had heard Falcon's questions, he didn't let on. He was so amazing. Sometimes, at the most unexpected moments, it took Dillion's breath. No one had ever cared for him like Beck. Not even Dillion's parents had done the things Beck did. He never complained or acted as if Dillion was too high maintenance. In fact, Dillion never had to ask for anything at all. Beck was always there, anticipating Dillion's every need and doing everything to make Dillion happy. Not falling in love with Beck wasn't an option. He was too perfect. Maybe that was why Dillion hadn't shown Beck the real him. While losing Beck might kill Dillion, having Beck look at him with disgust definitely would be the end of Dillion's life. His heart would never survive it. Even though he knew—at some point—he had built Beck one hell of a pedestal to fall from, Dillion hadn't found a single fault in the guy. He had looked. Hard. God knew he hadn't wanted to fall this deep when Beck didn't know everything. Beck hadn't given him a choice.

Dillion found himself urging Beck from his knee, luring him in for a kiss. Beck waited until the last second before dragging Dillion's scarf down, ensuring no one caught sight of Dillion as he claimed Dillion's lips. He had only meant for it to be a quick kiss. Dillion wasn't trying for a major public display of affection. It was Beck. He tasted too damn good and Dillion's heart was engaged. Their kiss turned carnal really fucking fast, making Dillion grateful his thick coat kept his erection hidden.

A loud cheer came from Falcon and he jumped them for a tackle hug. "You guys are so fucking cute. It makes me want to believe in true love. I don't, but you make me want to."

Beck re-covered Dillion's face with the scarf. His hungry stare held Dillion's for a moment longer before he gave Falcon his attention. "What are we doing now?"

Falcon booped noses with Beck because he was crazy like that. "You, my sexy new friend, are taking this one home," he said, pointing Dillion's way. "Because he needs all the loving, and I'm going to get drunk."

Beck's mouth lifted in one corner as he stared at Dillion. "Sounds like a solid plan."

Just like that, Dillion couldn't wait to get home.

BECK BIT HIS TONGUE ALL THE WAY HOME. HE made it until Dillion's back was cradled against his chest while jets and bubbles swirled around them. Dillion made a humming noise—like he was the happiest man on the planet. Beck broke.

"Why does everyone keep asking if I've seen the real you?"

Dillion's muscles tensed and immediately relaxed. He didn't answer right away. "I guess, to most, I'm a bit high maintenance and needy."

Outrage slammed into Beck's chest. "That's not true."

Dillion shrugged. "Actually, it is. I just think—for whatever reason—you don't see what everyone else does. Or it doesn't bother you like it does other people." He rolled and straddled Beck's hips, taking him from semi-erect to rock hard in an instant. "I always want you with me," he said, shifting closer until their erections bumped. "You do everything for me." He brushed his lips across Beck's and lowered his voice. "I'm demanding."

Beck forgot his earlier aggravation. Dillion's perfect ass filled his hands. He hauled Dillion closer, ensuring their cocks moved against each other. "You never ask me for anything. Everything I do, I do because I can't stop. You give me everything. I have nothing to offer."

An adorable burst of irritation crossed Dillion's features. "That's bullshit."

Beck's eyebrows rose. Until it happened, Beck didn't realize he didn't really hear Dillion curse often. It was adorable. A chuckle sneaked out. "You're sexy when you're angry. Of course, you're always hot."

Dillion's enraged expression melted away, turning into a blush. He looked away as if embarrassed by Beck's praise. "I don't like it when you talk bad about yourself."

"What should I do instead?" Beck ensured each word dripped with insinuation.

Each time Beck thought he couldn't get harder, Dillion did something else. He bit his lip, looking shy. Beck fought a growl at Dillion's sexy expression. No one had ever gotten so deep beneath his skin. Dillion's gorgeous green eyes slid back his way. His blush deepened. "I'd very much love for you to make love to me."

He would give Dillion anything, but that was one thing Dillion never had to ask for. He was at Dillion's service. Always.

DESPITE TELLING HIMSELF HE WOULDN'T JUMP Beck the second they got home, Dillion failed. He would like to think he would have succeeded if not for Beck asking questions that Dillion really didn't want to answer. Even though he was running with the belief he was distracting Beck, Dillion knew it was more than that. He wanted Beck. Now. Hard. He could tell Falcon had loved Beck. Falcon hated everyone. That only further proved Beck was every bit as amazing as Dillion believed. It wasn't all in his head. He wasn't just lonely. Beck was perfect. Dillion needed Beck inside him. Beck stared back at him with the same hunger. That was addicting. He felt special. Irreplaceable. No one had ever made him feel like this.

"We should go to bed."

A smirk pulled at Dillion's lips. He blatantly stroked Beck's cock. "Or I could keep you right here."

"You don't want that, baby. Trust me. It sounds fun, but—realistically—it's not. Water gets thrust into places it's got to come back out. It's not anywhere near as sexy as you'd think."

Dillion hadn't thought of that and definitely didn't want it. "You're right." While giggling like a kid, Dillion shot from the tub. The air was freezing compared to their bath. Dillion grabbed the only towel they had brought with them and ran for his room. Thankfully, Falcon hadn't come back yet, but Beck still had to make the walk, dripping and freezing. Uncaring of how messy things would be later, Dillion leapt into bed and crawled beneath the covers still wet. He expected a disgruntled Beck would be a little slower. Instead, before he could get settled, a soaked and rock-hard Beck tackled him, squishing him face down on the bed. A loud peal of laughter bounced from the bedroom walls as Beck stole his towel.

They struggled for control, wrestling beneath the covers like kids. Beck let him win. With Beck pinned to the bed, Dillion kissed every place he could reach. His cheeks hurt from smiling. Dillion stroked Beck's cock and balls before dipping lower and fingering his asshole. A sound filled the air that had pre-cum dripping from Dillion's erection. With wicked intent in his heart, Dillion turned and straddled Beck's waist. With his back to Beck, he had control of Dillion's dick. He could do whatever he wanted. He played, rubbing their cocks together, enjoying the sight of their crowns kissing. He didn't care if he was being silly. Dillion loved the vision they presented, delicate skin brushing delicate skin. A small tube of lube came sailing over Dillion's shoulder. A chuckle escaped Dillion as he went for it. He had forgotten they had gotten a delivery of fun stuff.

With his bottom lip held between his teeth, Dillion squeezed the shiny liquid onto Beck's cock before massaging. He had Beck's dick soaking wet. Slick. Dillion moved lower, coating Beck's balls too, because he could. He was in control. Not even Beck could see him. Dillion kept going. Beck's thighs fell open for him, giving him silent permission. Dillion easily slipped a finger inside Beck's hole with the lube slickening his hands. A gasp sounded behind him, making Dillion's dick twitch. He watched as a drop of pre-cum leaked from Beck's cock. All of Beck's cum was his.

Dillion fisted Beck's erection, holding him in place as he moved lower, positioning himself over Beck's dick. Beck stroked his hips and back as Dillion impaled himself, taking Beck deep. His eyes fell closed. He was home.

With his hands braced on Beck's upper thighs, Dillion rode Beck's cock. With his back to Beck, Dillion found himself turning wilder by the second. He let Beck hear his pleasure as he took Beck's dick as hard and as fast as he wanted it. The sounds Beck made—like he had never been more turned on—had

Dillion's every inhibition falling away. With his head thrown back, Dillion fucked his fist while taking every inch. He was crazed with the need to feel Beck even once this was over. Dillion wanted to wake up tomorrow and know Beck had been there. He wanted to smile knowingly with every twinge.

"Goddamn, Dillion. That's it, baby. Ride me. Oh, God. Take what you want."

Dillion barely heard a word. His heartbeat and gasps filled his ears. All he knew was what he felt. When it came to Beck, Dillion felt everything. It was way more than physical. He hadn't known love making could be so powerful. Everything he had done in the past hadn't really been about him. Beck gave Dillion permission to be as selfish as he wanted, and in the end, what Dillion wanted the most was to please Beck. The funny thing was, making Beck happy made him happy too. Sometimes, it was like they were one person. One soul.

Dillion's balls drew up tight. Beck's fingers dug into Dillion's hips. He growled. The sound punched Dillion in the gut. An orgasm slammed into him, stealing his breath. He gasped as he ground down on Beck, taking his pleasure. He sucked air.

"Oh, fuck." Beck shook beneath him as if Dillion had completely rocked him.

Dillion found himself desperately changing directions and crawling up Beck's body, needing his kiss. That was the gist of things, Dillion realized as their tongues met. Beck was completely necessary to him. That meant, eventually, he would have to show Beck the real him. There was no avoiding it.

FIVE

MASON KNEW he should stay away. That was the thing about Dillion—Mason never kept his distance. Everything he did was for Dillion. Sometimes, that meant winning him. Other times, Mason was trying to hurt him. There was rarely a middle ground between them. They were a sickness. An ugly yet beautiful addiction Mason couldn't shake.

Even as he headed to Dillion's door, Mason knew he was making a mistake. Nothing good could come of him showing up here... unless something good came of him coming here. He never knew which way things would go when it came to Dillion. From day to day, he might love Mason or hate him. Either way, Mason had never tasted so much passion anywhere else.

After five minutes of knocking and ringing the bell, most people would have given up. Mason knew Dillion. He was purposely making Mason wait, but Dillion would give in. Dillion always gave in. He fought a smirk when the door swung wide. Until he caught sight of the man on the other side. Then, irritation owned Mason. Falcon had the same build as Dillion. That was where their similarities ended. Whereas Dillion was the sweetest person on Earth, Falcon was not.

"Who are you?"

Mason tried not to roll his eyes. "Mason. You're Falcon. We've met."

Falcon's eyebrows rose. He dropped his gaze to Mason's feet and openly eyed Mason's entire body before meeting his stare again. His unusual light gray eyes held Mason fascinated. "Since you know my name, I won't call you a liar, but it's also possible you've seen my YouTube channel." He shrugged. "You're pretty forgettable, so..."

"Wow." Even Mason heard the sarcasm in his voice. "You're not, but that's only because I remember how big of an ass you are. I had to throw two of your bodyguards out of the club I manage."

There wasn't an ounce of recognition or even interest in Falcon's eyes. He looked bored as hell.

"Nope. Don't remember. If I had security with me, it wasn't for me. Must've been people I hired to keep Dillion safe. So, what do you want?"

Mason swallowed his temper. "Well, I mean, this is Dillion's house. Obviously, I'm here to see him."

"Sorry, dude. Being as how it's eight in the morning and he isn't ninety, he's still in bed."

"You're up. What's your excuse?"

Falcon smirked. It made him twice as hot and Mason hated that he noticed. "I haven't been to bed yet."

Mason fought the urge to roll his eyes. Only the young bragged about being that stupid. "All right. If you'll move aside, I'll go wake up Dillion. This is kind of important."

"No." Falcon didn't look angry. In fact, his expression didn't change at all. Mason wasn't sure he had actually heard the denial. It was possible it had been Mason's imagination.

"Excuse me?"

Falcon shook his head. "Surely you're not so old you're deaf already. I said no. I'm not stepping aside."

"Look, I don't know who you think you are, but this isn't your house, and I'm sure you're aware I could easily move you out of my way. Choose the easy path here. Step aside."

To Mason's surprise, Falcon laughed. Mason had to take a breath at the sexiness of the sound. Before Mason could recover, Falcon's eyes hardened. "I take it back; you haven't seen my channel, or you'd recognize the puddle of shit you just stepped in. If you think you've got the balls to move me, try it, fucker."

Mason blinked. It was like he stared at someone he had never seen. He opened his mouth, ready to blast Falcon for stepping into a man's sized shoes and getting ready to get his ass handed to him. Dillion appeared at Falcon's back. The words died in Mason's throat.

"It's okay, angel. I've got it. He doesn't know who he just challenged."

Falcon didn't step away immediately. He eyed Mason a moment longer, looking ready to fight before finally stepping aside. Mason's gaze slid Dillion's way. His irritation slipped away, and his heart squeezed in his chest, the way it always did when Dillion was around. It didn't help that Dillion's hair was a mess, and he wore tiny shorts and a long baggy t-shirt, making him look like he wore a dress. He was so fucking beautiful no matter what he wore. Mason had so many unfulfilled fantasies when it came to Dillion. He had been dying, trying to wait until Dillion turned eighteen to claim him. Unfortunately, all he ever seemed to do was hurt Dillion instead. Mason swallowed. "Is it okay if I come in? I have some stuff I need to say."

Dillion backed up enough to give Mason room to pass. Mason's feet froze to the ground when the move left him an open view of the same guy who carried Dillion away the last time he had seen Dillion. He sat at the kitchen table with Falcon eating breakfast. Mason's gaze slid back Dillion's way. "Maybe you could step outside instead? Or we could go to your room..."

Dillion rolled his eyes. "For heaven's sake. If you have something to say, come in and say it. It's too cold for this."

With no other choice left to him, he stepped inside. He decided to brazen things out. Mason kept his gaze straight ahead, not meeting anyone's stare as he headed through the kitchen door and intent on hitting the bedroom.

"Living room," Dillion barked at his back, stopping Mason before he made his getaway.

Mason decided to take it. At least he would have Dillion alone. He veered into the living room. The first chair he came to, he sat. When he focused again on an irritated-looking Dillion, his heart screamed for Dillion to close the space between them. Dillion stopped feet away with his arms crossed over his chest. Mason wondered if he was protecting his heart. God knew Mason had broken it enough times. "I love you."

"Fuck you," Dillion said, dragging out the words. His eyes flashed with fury. "There's not a chance in hell you know what love is and still treat me the way you always have. When you love someone, their feelings always come first. The only person you love is yourself."

"You're more than twenty years younger than me, Dillion. I know you've been grown your whole life, but stop blaming me for wanting you to at least get to eighteen, for fuck's sake. People already act like I'm the world's biggest perv for messing with you to begin with."

Dillion scrubbed at his forehead, looking beyond frustrated. His shoulders rose and fell on a deep breath before he focused on Mason again. "None of this matters. I'm with Beck now. This visit, whatever it is, it's too late."

Mason wanted to scream and break shit. Dillion

was the biggest flake. "I'm who you've got history with. Not some guy you just met."

Dillion shook his head. "We didn't just meet. In fact, you're currently disrespecting his home by being here. I think you should go."

Mason blinked. He had never met anyone so ridiculous. "People don't fall in and out of love as fast as you do and expect it to be real. This is your home. You're the one who worked for it. Moving some guy in who'll be gone in a week doesn't make this his home." Mason shook his head. "Are you even listening to yourself? I'm the one who's been around the world for you. If anyone's getting disrespected right now, it's me. I should be able to carry you to bed right now because I fucking earned that right. Yet, I'm confined to the living room while getting accused of disrespecting someone else's house. What the actual fuck, Dillion?" With every word Mason spoke, his temper rose a little more. He didn't want to care about this spoiled, insane brat, but here he was. Mason couldn't help how he felt.

"It's time for you to go," Falcon said, appearing next to Dillion. "I get that Dillion hoped to give you a chance to apologize or whatever, but unlike him, I know men like you never see your faults."

Beck moved to stand behind Dillion. He

massaged Dillion's shoulders, looking like he had Dillion's back. Dillion leaned back against Beck's chest, visibly seeking shelter against Mason in Beck's hold.

Falcon motioned toward the door. "I won't repeat myself. Beck's a better person than me. He won't set you on your ass the way you deserve, but I will." Falcon's features hardened a little more with every word, making him sexier by the minute. "The way you talk to Dillion, you make me fucking sick. Go home and look in the mirror. No one here needs a pathetic forty-year-old child who can't keep his dick in his pants then faults the person he's supposed to love for his weak character. Don't you have a man at home already?"

Temper fully engaged; Mason came to his feet. He smirked. "I thought you didn't remember me. Now you know everything, right?" His voice rose with every word. If this boy wanted his ass handed to him, Mason had time. Beck had turned Dillion to face him. He cupped Dillion's face and spoke in low tones, telling him things that made Mason's stomach churn and his mood darken. Mason wasn't that person. He didn't sweet talk anyone and Dillion had never been the type to want it. Beck towed Dillion closer and touched his lips to Dillion's forehead.

Everything inside Mason snapped. Dillion belonged to him. He took two steps in Dillion's direction, intent on taking what was his. In a flash, the room spun, and the ceiling stared at him. He blinked, trying to decide what happened. Before he fully grasped that he was on his back, he was back on his feet and moving toward the door with no help from his own body. His knee hit a kitchen chair, knocking it over.

"If your stupid ass hurt that chair, I'll send you a bill," Falcon spat against his ear as he hauled Mason toward the door. Falcon's touch didn't hurt. More than anything, Mason was beyond confused as to why he couldn't control his own body. Falcon had him in a hold Mason couldn't break and easily maneuvered Mason like Mason didn't outweigh him by a hundred pounds. The guy didn't even sound winded as he tossed Mason out the back door. Mason scrambled to stay upright. He spun.

Falcon blocked the open doorway, looking ready to kill. "If you come back here, I'll snap your fucking legs, understood?" He slammed the door, shutting Mason out of Dillion's life.

All he could do was stare at the closed door while trying to figure out what happened. Cold air blasted him as the wind picked up. With his heart in tatters, Mason headed for his truck, but he couldn't bring himself to leave. He didn't know why he had said so many awful things to Dillion. Mason didn't know why he always did. He scrubbed at his forehead. Something about Dillion made him act in a way he didn't with anyone else. It was like the guy made him half insane. He knew he should stay away, but Mason couldn't. It was like he was addicted to eating poison. Even though he knew Dillion was killing him, Mason couldn't stop coming back for more.

Mason dug out his phone, intent on texting Dillion. Maybe he could convince him to come outside and try again. Instead, Mason opened his web browser and typed in Falcon's name. Countless results appeared, but all Mason wanted was his bio. There was something about the guy.

Former Hollywood stuntman Falcon Vaspiro is more than meets the eye. Owner of World Life Street Fights, a popular YouTube channel that follows the mixed martial arts expert from secret venue to secret venue as he takes on different opponents, is only twenty-two years old, but he is known all over the world for his skill.

Mason stared into space without finishing the article. He had to admit that was fucking hot. Maybe he would go back inside and get his ass handed to him again. After all, Mason adored the crazy ones.

DILLION LOOKED A WRECK. BECK WAS PRETTY sure Dillion might fall apart at any second, but he also didn't believe it was all on Mason. It was like he was internalizing everything, finding faults in himself. Beck didn't know how to fight the voices inside Dillion's head. He had noticed this happened to Dillion occasionally. His mind got the better of him and dark thoughts ruled his decisions. Beck was scared of what Dillion would do after this one.

Falcon reappeared after tossing out Mason. He looked completely calm and collected as if it was a normal day for him. "You should've let me kick his ass before he made it into the house."

Dillion nodded without meeting anyone's gaze. "I know. I always make stupid decisions."

Beck fought an internal scream. He didn't know how to fight what he couldn't see, and Dillion always kept his thoughts hidden.

"Don't start that," Falcon said, sounding understanding. "That's your mom talking."

"Is it okay if I have some time alone?"

Beck took it in the chest. Through everything, Dillion had never asked him to go away before. "If that's what you want." Even Beck heard the dead note to his voice.

Dillion's gaze moved to his. He touched Beck's cheek. "I'm okay. It's all right. I just need to be alone, okay? My thoughts get dark and I don't want to say things I don't mean and regret them. Sometimes, I just need to step away from myself."

"It's cool," Falcon said, slapping Beck across the back. "This'll give me a chance to steal Beck and win him to the dark side, so he doesn't take away my key." Even though Falcon was smiling, there was something dark in his eyes. Beck saw his chance. Falcon knew Dillion like no one else did. If anyone could tell him how to break through these dark moods, it was Falcon.

"Yeah," Beck said, flashing Dillion a reassuring smile he didn't feel. "I'm sure Falcon and I can find something to get into while you decompress from whatever that bullshit was." He towed Dillion forward because he couldn't leave without making sure Dillion understood Mason couldn't touch them. Beck brushed his lips across Dillion's and Dillion came back for more. That small concession was enough to steady Beck. He could give Dillion some space. "I have my phone," Beck reminded him. "If you need anything or if Mason comes back, call me. We'll come right back."

"Yep," Falcon said behind him. "We're a call away." He squeezed Beck's shoulder, urging him toward the door. Beck went, fighting the urge to turn back every step.

By the time he was sitting in the passenger seat of Falcon's Hellcat, Beck was certain he would snap a tendon any second. Falcon started the car and kicked up the heat, but he made no move to leave.

"No fucking way am I going anywhere and leaving that Mason douche an opening to come back while Dillion is unprotected." Falcon sounded pissed and deadly. Nothing like he had inside. Beck's head snapped around. Falcon stared at the house and chewed the side of his nail. He looked ready to explode. "Fucking bastard. As if Dillion doesn't have enough voices in his head, telling him he's stupid, crazy, and unlovable. The last goddamn thing he needs is someone like that motherfucker coming around."

Beck nodded, because he didn't know what to do. He felt like he had a lot to say, but his tongue wouldn't work. "I don't know what to do." Beck didn't know where the confession came from. He didn't want to admit to any weaknesses, but Beck didn't know how to be someone Dillion could love. There was a piece of Dillion that Beck couldn't reach, and he didn't know how to fight what he couldn't see.

"I'm not surprised." At Falcon's words, Beck stared hard at the man who'd known Dillion almost his entire life. He felt it in his gut that Falcon knew how to reach Dillion. Falcon kept his gaze locked on the house. "Being raised by Hollywood isn't something you can describe, especially when you have a mom like Dillion's. Someone who didn't care what her son had to do or what happened to him as long as he made the money she wanted. If I ever have kids, you can bet your life I'll keep them as far away from the childhood we had as possible. It destroys people. In the end, some people turn out like me—cold and hard. Other people, they turn out like Dillion—a mess." Beck opened his mouth to defend Dillion. Falcon held up a hand, stopping him. "That doesn't mean he isn't the greatest person on the planet, because I know he is, but what he gives others isn't what he keeps for himself, and that's what I'm talking about." Falcon looked his way. "He needs you. More than anything, he needs you to love him the way he is. No one gives him that."

"I do." Even Beck heard the steady confidence in his words. It was more than an affirmation. It was a promise. Beck didn't see a mess. He saw someone who needed love as much as he did, and Beck did love him.

Falcon held his stare. His eerie-colored eyes seemed to see all the way to Beck's soul. "Yeah. I know you do. My fear is that Mason won't give up and he'll finally end up doing exactly what he hoped to do today—drive you away."

Beck refused to as much as blink as he held Falcon's gaze. "That's not happening. I know something Mason can't see."

"I imagine you know a million things Mason will never know."

Beck couldn't help but smile at the evil note to Falcon's voice. "Dillion loves me."

Falcon smiled. "I know he does. That's why you're not leaving. I know that Dillion thinks he wants space right now, but really, he needs me to make myself scarce and you to remind him Mason is full of shit. He's had a few minutes to break shit. Go inside and fix him. I'll sit out here a little while longer and make sure Mason doesn't come back."

There was no way Beck could express how grateful he was for Falcon. He had been fighting the urge to rush the house since he had stepped outside. It mattered that Falcon agreed he should. That meant Beck wasn't insane. Dillion didn't need to be alone right now. "Thank you."

Falcon waved off his gratitude. "Go take care of our boy. That's all that matters."

Beck nodded and leapt from the car before Falcon thought twice. He had seen Falcon fight. The last thing Beck wanted was to be dragged away from Dillion. Still, as he reached the back door, Beck's steps slowed. He hoped Dillion realized this was for the best too.

With a deep breath for courage, Beck opened the door. "I know you want me gone..." Beck said as he came through the door, readying his argument before he even set eyes on Dillion. The words died on his lips as he set eyes on Dillion.

Dillion stared back at Beck over the mouth of the wine bottle he had obviously been turning up. Beck hadn't been gone that long. It didn't matter. Dillion had undergone a complete transformation. His face was the same, except for the tracks of tears down both cheeks, but he wore a short white dress that stopped right below his ass cheeks. It was formfitting and showed off Dillion's zero fat body. White thigh-high stocking covered his legs, and he wore white Mary Jane style dress shoes.

Beck immediately sat in the same chair Mason had turned over minutes earlier. Beck's knees didn't give out. He had to hide his immediate erection. Beck was convinced he had never been harder in his life, even though Dillion looked like he had gotten busted murdering someone. He tried to hide, but there was nowhere to go. Instead, he held the wine bottle in front of him, as if that would stop Beck from seeing what he wore. Beck shook off his shock.

"Is this the real you that everyone's been asking about?"

Dillion swiped at his face. He nodded, as if he couldn't speak. He kept swiping away his tears and losing the battle when more streamed down his face.

"Come here." Even Beck heard the rough edge to his voice.

Dillion's gaze shot to his. His eyes were blood red and so was the tip of his nose, and he was still so goddamn beautiful.

"Come here," Beck repeated when Dillion didn't move.

Dillion crossed the room, looking like he was walking to his death. He stopped inches from Beck. Beck pried the bottle from Dillion's hands and set it aside. He motioned for Dillion to turn around. Beck needed to see the entire outfit. Dillion slowly turned. Beck flipped up the back of the skirt because he had to know what was beyond the thigh-high stockings. He nearly came as he caught sight of the white cotton virginal-looking panties beneath.

"Dear God," Beck breathed, hearing the lust in his voice and unable to mask it. "You're beautiful."

At his praise, Dillion slowly turned back to face him. He twisted his fingers while chewing his bottom lip. Dillion looked scared to hope.

Beck's hands found Dillion's hips. He drew the man closer while holding his stare. "You should let me take off those panties so you can sit in my lap."

Dillion visibly swallowed. "You don't have to pretend to like me," Dillion said, sounding wrecked. "I just need to be me... sometimes, especially when everything else feels wrong. I don't have to do it in front of you. It's okay if you need me to pretend like it doesn't happen."

Beck stood and got in Dillion's space. He held Dillion's hand against his erection while forcing Dillion to hold his stare. "Tell me I'm pretending," Beck dared. "From the first time I set eyes on you, I've wanted you. Not just sexually or for who I thought you are or might do for me. I craved a taste of that fire I saw in your outrage at the unfairness of life. You're mine and you're perfect. Stop letting what other people think dictate how you see me." Beck stabbed at his chest, completely losing his temper. He had held his tongue while Mason pulled his shit, but he was tired of being quiet. Dillion belonged to him. The hope in Dillion's eyes kept Beck's confessions flowing. He had known Dillion needed more from him. Beck just hadn't known how to give him what he needed. Now Beck knew. He wouldn't stop until Dillion understood Beck wanted everything about him. "Tell me how I can prove that I'm so fucking proud to be with you. I'm ready to blow at the slightest brush of your hand right now, but if you need me to take you to dinner instead, to prove how goddamn beautiful you look right now, then let's go. Let me show you off to the world. Stop running from me. I'm not ashamed."

"I am." The whispered confession shattered Beck's heart. "Mason said people will laugh at me if I go out like this."

A growl escaped Beck before he could stop it. His temper snapped. "I don't give a fuck what Mason thinks. Why do you care so much about him and what he believes? He doesn't love you. I do. In all my days, I've never been more tired of hearing someone's name. For fuck's sake, why can't you let him go and see the person standing right in front of you? Do you think I don't know what it's like to have an ex fuck you up? I do. My ex used to tell me all the time how boring I am. Maybe I'm not exciting. Maybe that's why I haven't done a good enough job of proving myself. It's possible I'm just not enough for anyone. I'm not enough for you."

Dillion didn't cower from Beck's temper. In fact, he stared at Beck like he hung on every word. When he spoke, his voice sounded small but steady. "I was going to say, I don't care if people laugh at me. But I don't want them to laugh at you because I love you. It's my job to keep you safe. You're everything to me."

Beck's mind blanked. He had spent so much time trying to find a way to tell Dillion he loved him, he never expected Dillion would say it back. Beck's hands slipped beneath Dillion's skirt, finding the globes of his ass. He lifted, leaving Dillion no other choice than to cling to Beck's shoulders and wrap his legs around Beck's waist to keep his balance. "If you love me, then why are you crying over Mason?"

The adorable outrage on Dillion's face might have made Beck laugh under different circumstances. "I'm not crying over Mason. I'm crying because Mason made me realize I'm disappointing you."

Beck shook his head and sat. He held on to Dillion, keeping the man straddled across his lap. Beck had no intention of letting Dillion get away. "You've never, not once disappointed me. To me, you're perfect. I've never been happy before you. Being with you, it's been like heaven to me. Please don't let anyone else's voice in your head. Just me. I'm so fucking happy here with you." He dipped his head and kissed Dillion's collarbone and inhaled his sweet scent. "I love you so much. You're all that exists for me."

Dillion kissed him. It was so gentle, it melted Beck's heart. "I'm so in love with you," Dillion whispered between kisses. "You make everything so beautiful. I didn't expect you, but I'm so glad I found you."

"Awww, shit, y'all," Falcon said, coming through the door with his gaze locked on his phone. Dillion didn't jump from Beck's lap and Beck held tight so he wouldn't try. "Did you two know you're engaged?" He looked up as he turned his phone their way. His expression went through a dozen changes as he realized what he had walked into.

Beck stared at the face of Falcon's phone while

Dillion chewed his ear as if they were alone. There was a picture of Beck on one knee at the fight. He had been tying Dillion's shoe, but it damn sure looked like he was proposing.

"It sounds like I said yes," Dillion whispered against the shell of Beck's ear. Beck prayed Dillion didn't stand up and show the room Beck's erection.

Falcon went back to staring at his phone. "Seriously, if you scroll through the pictures, it looks dead up like you popped the question, Dillion said yes, and I was celebrating while congratulating you both. These pics are pretty damning." Falcon looked up again, seemingly unbothered by Dillion's open attempt at seducing Beck in the middle of the kitchen. "By the way, you look pretty, Dillion. I haven't seen you like this in a long time."

"He is beautiful, isn't he?" Beck agreed. Dillion kissed his cheek. Beck's heart needed everything. "You know, I feel a little guilty. Like I'm making a liar out of someone." He turned his head and captured Dillion's lips for a quick kiss before pressing his forehead to Dillion's and holding his stare. "Do you remember when you said I could probably ask you for anything? You should marry me."

Dillion flashed him an adorable smile. "Someday."

"I'll take it." Beck wasn't going anywhere. Tomorrow or fifty years from now, Beck would feel the same. He turned his head to find Falcon staring at them, wearing a huge smile. He looked between them for a moment before the intimacy of the moment he had interrupted seemed to finally dawn on him. "Oh. You two should probably be alone. I just saw the article and had to tell you. As you were," he said, heading back outside.

Dillion's body shook with laughter. Beck held him tighter. He was Beck's heart. Beck was fine to sit like this all day, ignoring his hard on, and holding his sweet baby. Then, Dillion licked the shell of his ear. He forgot about everything except what Dillion always did to his body. Dillion was sexy and sexual. He always rocked Beck to his core. Dillion acted as if making love to Beck was the greatest experience of his life. Not only did being with Dillion stroke Beck's ego—he got that he won the fucking love lottery with Dillion—Dillion also left him breathless. He had never been so whipped. Nor did Beck give a damn if the whole world knew it. In fact, he wanted the whole world to know, so they would understand he would kill to keep Dillion forever. They were forever.

Beck slipped his hands beneath Dillion's skirt and palmed his ass. Dillion licked and sucked at Beck's ear while Beck leaked in his jeans. He already knew he wouldn't last long if he ever got inside Dillion. It felt like it wouldn't happen today with his impatience at an all-time high.

"There's a real possibility Falcon will burst in again. He gets bored easily."

Beck thought he might cry. Dillion was teasing him while saying they wouldn't get to play because they weren't alone.

Dillion stood and held out his hand. "Come on, gorgeous. Let's lock ourselves away so I can lick you all over."

Beck scrambled to his feet and accepted Dillion's hand. "Will you leave on the shoes and stockings?"

Dillion glanced over his shoulder with his bottom lip held between his teeth. He looked happy. Beck wanted nothing else. At the doorway to their bedroom, Dillion turned and walked backward into the room while holding Beck's hands. Beck couldn't see anything else but the green of Dillion's eyes. There was love and then there was this sickness that lived under Beck's skin. He had never been happier in his life than he had been since meeting Dillion.

Beck kicked the door closed behind them. Dillion led him to the bed. Beck sat and tugged Dillion to stand between his knees. The dress had a row of tiny buttons down the front. It looked daunting—like it would take Beck forever to get Dillion out of his outfit. Before he could decide what to do, Dillion pushed, shoving him on to his back. He peeled off Beck's jeans and underwear in an attack that didn't give Beck time to do anything but take it. Then he dropped to his knees between Beck's. Beck tried to sit up because he wanted to watch. Dillion dove in face first, rolling Beck's eyes back in his head and stopping him from concentrating on anything but trying not to immediately come.

Dillion pushed Beck's thighs apart and sucked his balls. He tongued Beck's hole and deep throated his cock like a porn star. Sounds tore from Beck's throat he didn't know he could make. If Dillion asked him to rob a bank in that moment, Beck would have agreed to anything as long as Dillion didn't stop. Beck was a complete mess. He had never begged for anything in his life. Without an ounce of shame, he begged Dillion for more.

"Dillion. Please, baby? Oh my god. Don't stop."

He held tight to the comforter beneath him, seeking purchase. "Fuck. The things you do to me. You mess with my head. I've never wanted anyone or loved anyone as much as I do you."

Dillion sucked hard and Beck exploded. His whole body shook from the power of his orgasm. Dillion didn't stop sucking, going for every drop of cum while Beck twitched and barely clung to sanity. He babbled things he forgot the instant they left his mouth. There was only one thing he knew for certain—when he got back the ability to use his arms, Dillion would sit on his face in his pretty white dress and ride Beck into this same level of insanity even if Beck had to die in the pursuit. There was no middle ground here. Dillion deserved the world. Beck would give it to him.

SIX

THEIR HOUSE BECAME a haven Dillion never expected. Dillion was freer than he had ever been, even when he had lived alone, thanks to Beck insisting Dillion dress the way he wanted more and more often. After Dillion took some time to look closer at things, he realized he should have trusted Beck would accept him from the beginning. Beck had never done anything to deserve Dillion's distrust. The fault was in Dillion. He had let Mason twist him into someone insecure. Dillion had spent so much time treating Mason better than he treated himself that he had forgotten how to be cherished. He was still learning. Sometimes, he still failed. Thankfully, Beck had the patience of a saint. He was exactly the balm Dillion's soul needed.

Dillion poured coffee over cream, watching it turn the perfect shade of brown. A smile pulled at the corners of his mouth as Beck's lips skimmed his shoulder.

"Good morning, sexy. The bed was getting cold without you."

Dillion stirred the coffee before slowly turning Beck's way, trying not to spill a drop. "I wanted to bring you breakfast in bed, but you were too quick for me. I managed to make coffee, though."

Beck stared at the cup like Dillion handed him the keys to a new car. "This is perfect. Thank you. I don't need anything else." Beck's gaze lifted to Dillion's. Love stared at him. "Except a kiss," Beck added, taking the cup and setting it aside so he could hold Dillion.

Dillion slid his hands up Beck's chest before linking his fingers behind Beck's neck. Beck shuffled closer, backing him against the counter before dipping his head and nibbling on Dillion's bottom lip. Dillion chuckled at Beck's playfulness. Their home was full of happiness and peace. Love. Dillion didn't need or want anything else. The moment Beck finally deepened their kiss, the doorbell rang.

"Ugh," Dillion groaned.

Beck set him free to answer the door. Dillion

checked the peephole. For a moment, he stared in surprise at the man standing on the other side. He didn't shake off his shock enough to answer until Trace rang the bell again.

"Trace. Wow. I didn't even know you knew where I lived."

Trace was sexy, sensual, and charming. Everyone loved him, including Dillion. The young club owner was good to everyone, especially his much older husband. Dillion had a great deal of respect for his bravery. Trace eyed the short, pink silk robe Dillion wore. Not a hint of judgment marred his features. "Hey, darling. Is it okay if I come in?"

"Oh," Dillion said, shifting backward. "Sorry. Come in." In his surprise, he had forgotten his manners.

Trace's gaze swung Beck's way as he stepped inside. Beck set the coffee he had been sipping aside again and crossed the room with his hand extended. "I don't think we've officially met. I'm Beck."

"Nice to meet you," Trace said, hopping to meet Beck halfway and accept his handshake. "I'd heard a rumor that Dillion was hiding a gorgeous new addition to his home. I'm Trace. Owner of Incubus. We might've met a while back, but everything went to shit before I had a chance to introduce myself."

Beck had started blushing at the "gorgeous" remark and hadn't looked directly at Trace since. A wave of jealousy overcame Dillion. Trace was so much more of everything than Dillion. Then Beck looked past Trace and focused on Dillion. It was like their souls brushed. Beck stepped around Trace to take Dillion's hand.

Dillion held tight, feeling his jealousy melt away. He motioned toward the living room. "Would you like to sit down?"

Trace's light blue gaze moved between them. He looked curious, but he nodded and followed them into the living room. Trace chose the recliner, leaving the loveseat for Dillion and Beck. He waited until everyone was seated to speak. "I didn't mean to disturb you before you were up and going for the day."

Dillion waved off his apology as he curled his legs underneath him and leaned Beck's way. Beck tucked him beneath his arm. "We've gotten lazy lately. Since I haven't had any scheduled trips or anything, we've started sleeping in and staying in our pajamas all day. You probably could've waited until this afternoon and still caught us exactly like this." Dillion laughed as he made the confession.

The way Trace smiled warmed Dillion's heart.

He had always liked Trace. The guy was genuinely nice. His smile disappeared. "I haven't stopped feeling like a terrible person since the last time we spoke. Since I opened Club Incubus, you've done nothing but try to help, bringing in crowds and supporting the club's every event. For real, you've been an awesome friend. I shouldn't have told you not to come back."

Dillion's brow furrowed in confusion. "Yes, you should. That was the second time I've been in a fight there." A soft chuckle escaped Beck at the admission. Dillion patted his thigh and continued. "Club Incubus is your baby. As you said, you took a risk by letting me in before I turned eighteen. I know you did it because my being there brought in business, but still, I don't have many friends." Dillion stopped there because the more he spoke, the less he liked what he heard himself say. He had spent his whole life making friends by basically buying them. Beck was the only person who'd ever put up a fight, balking at the idea of Dillion feeling used by him.

As if Beck read his mind, he brought Dillion's hand to his mouth and kissed his knuckles. "Stop, baby," he said for Dillion's ears only. "You're amazing and loved."

Dillion's eyes stung. He swiped at his face. "I love you."

"I demoted Mason from manager," Trace said, bringing Dillion's gaze back his way. "He's also no longer allowed at the club on Friday nights unless there's a dire need. He knows I value our friendship, and he fucked up by attacking Beck. While I'd appreciate it if you stuck to Friday nights until Mason and you can find a way to coexist peacefully, I would love for you to come back. Like I said, you're my friend. I wish I'd intervened sooner, because you didn't deserve to have someone like Mason in your life. In my defense, I've had a lot going on, and I didn't realize how bad things had gotten."

The lump in Dillion's throat wouldn't let him speak. He took a breath, trying harder. "It's not your fault that I didn't know how to save myself."

"Don't say that," Trace said, sounding truly upset. "I've seen you fiercely stand up for others. The way you were there for Lane when Walker was down, that's who you are. You give too much of yourself, and it's not because you're weak or desperate. It's because you're good." His gaze slid Beck's way before he focused on Dillion once more. "I'm so damn glad you've met someone who obviously treats you the way you deserve. I'm glad you realized you deserve it."

"Dillion has always known he deserves to be treated like the goddess he is," Beck said, bringing everyone's gaze his way. He looked hard and like the hero Dillion had fallen in love with. "He just hasn't wanted to beg anyone to treat him the way they should." Beck's expression didn't soften, but Dillion's heart did with every word. "Normal people don't only care about someone when that someone can do something for them. Normal people try to find ways to make their friends lives better because they care. No one should have to earn normal."

"I love you." The words burst from Dillion as he stared at Beck. Beck wasn't particularly vocal. He was quiet strength. Steady. Never before had Dillion been so sure of anyone having his back. Six months or fifty years from now, Dillion knew Beck would be there, standing with him.

Beck kissed Dillion's knuckles again. "I love you too," he said against the back of Dillion's hand. He moved Dillion's hand to his chest and held him there against his heartbeat, even as he spoke to Trace. "Thank you for finding a way to keep Dillion safe when he's visiting your club," Beck said, focusing on

Trace once more. "It means a lot to me, and I know Dillion misses his friends."

In truth, Dillion hadn't thought about anyone lately. He had been pretty content to be right here, but Beck was right. Dillion would miss Summer, Lane, and the rest before long. He was damn glad to know he could go to Incubus without seeing Mason.

"You don't have to thank me for that," Trace said, waving off Beck's gratitude. "I should've done something sooner. I knew Mason had gotten out of control, but Walker was undergoing treatment for a brain tumor and Lane was caring for him. Hunter and I started a new club on the east coast, so I needed Mason to do right by me while the rest of us had our hands full." Trace made a helpless gesture that had Dillion's heart going out to him. "The last couple of years have been hectic. I guess I hoped he would get his shit together without me having to intervene, because God knows I don't have the time. But Walker's doing better, so he's going to come back in the management position. Lane plans to help out too since Walker and he are stuck together like glue. Things are getting better. I never meant for you to fall through the cracks while everything was going on. You matter to us too."

The lump was back in Dillion's throat. "I know.

That's why I've stayed away. I know you have a lot going on."

"We love you and want you, okay?"

The sincerity in Trace's voice was almost Dillion's undoing. Beck was probably the only person who fully understood how badly Dillion needed to be wanted for himself. No one, not even his parents, had wanted him for anything other than what he could do for them before he had started going to Incubus. Then Mason had stolen that from him. Without meeting Beck, Dillion might not have survived it. That wasn't him being dramatic. He was tired. Beck had saved him. Dillion wouldn't give him up. Not ever. Beck was his happy ever after. His everything.

EPILOGUE

IT NEVER FAILED that Dillion got stuck preparing some sort of food on Coral's show. At least he had Beck at his side this time. Proving he was the greatest of men, even though Dillion knew Beck was nervous about being on live TV, no one could look at him and tell it. He chopped the broccoli Coral set in front of him without complaint—the way Beck did everything.

"You know I don't usually talk to my guests about anything I read on the cover of gossip magazines, especially this particular magazine. However, I read that the two of you are engaged and I have to know if there's any truth to that."

Beck and Dillion exchanged a smile.

Dillion chose to answer. "You know I have a

special hatred for gossip columns. In this case, they actually got something right."

Coral bounced on her toes and clapped along with the audience. "Wow. This is so exciting. Beck, what made you decide to pop the question at a street fight?"

The way Coral said street fight bothered Dillion a little, but he got it. Dillion probably seemed like it wouldn't be his thing, but it was Falcon's and he loved Falcon. Dillion didn't give Beck a chance to answer, especially since Beck would either have to lie or admit he had only been tying Dillion's shoe at Falcon's fight. "Actually, that was all about me," Dillion said, still chopping his onion. "As many people know, Falcon Vaspiro is my oldest friend. Beck knew I would want Falcon to be there when he asked, and Falcon would want to be there too, so he dropped to one knee while he had the chance." It wasn't a total lie. "With that said, he asked me the next day at our home in Aspen in a more romantic setting. Not that it matters where it happened, of course. Falcon was actually there for both."

"You've really found yourself a keeper, Dillion," Coral said, sounding moved. "I've never dated anyone who cared about my friends or how they feel."

"We both love Falcon," Beck said with a shrug, finally getting a word in.

Dillion nodded. "And Falcon loves Beck."

"You two are so adorable, and we love when you join us. Don't we love it when Dillion joins us?" Coral asked the audience to another round of cheers. She chuckled. "That's why I wanted to give something back. You're always willing to drop by and help me out. I want to make sure your marriage starts out right. That's why I'm sending you two to Fiji for your honeymoon."

Dillion bounced in place. He could afford his own honeymoon, but he loved Coral, and it was such a nice thing to do. Dillion wanted to make sure she understood he appreciated the gesture. "Awww, Coral." He hugged her. She moved on to hug Beck too. "That's so nice."

With hugs out of the way, Coral went back to chopping next to them. "Tell us all the rest of your secrets. Who is the designer of this fabulous outfit you're wearing?"

Dillion automatically glanced down, even though he knew what he was wearing, and the long, flowy skirt was mostly covered by his apron. "Well, you know Omen from Slight Bastards, right?"

Coral nodded. "He was on the show a few months back."

"His husband, Keegan, recently started a fashion line for men like me," he said, waving dismissively toward his clothes. Even as Dillion fell into a description of Keegan's clothing line, Dillion recognized how far he had come and how free he was now. It was completely Beck's doing. Dillion wouldn't let that pass without acknowledgement. "Actually, it was Beck who read about Keegan's clothing line and convinced me to check it out. He's a rock. I'm probably the luckiest man alive for having found such a supportive partner. He's amazing."

Beck stared at Dillion as Dillion sang his praises and the truth struck Dillion. Beck needed Dillion's praise every bit as much as Dillion needed Beck's steady presence. Sometimes, Dillion felt like he took more than he gave when it came to Beck, but it wasn't true. They were a team, shoring up each other in a world that didn't always fit them. They were blessed to have met. They were absolutely perfect, and they always would be.

KEEP AN EYE OUT FOR THE NEXT BOOK IN THE Sugar Babies series, *Salty Baby*.

ABOUT THE AUTHOR

Charity Parkerson is an award winning and multi-published author with several companies. Born with no filter from her brain to her mouth, she decided to take this odd quirk and insert it in her characters.

*Eight-time Readers' Favorite Award Winner
    *2015 Passionate Plume Award Finalist
    *2013 Reviewers' Choice Award Winner
    *2012 ARRA Finalist for Favorite Paranormal Romance
    *Five-time winner of The Mistress of the Darkpath

Connect with her online:

--Join   my   street   team:
facebook.com/TeamCharityParkerson
    --Website: charityparkerson.com
    --Facebook:
facebook.com/authorCharityParkerson

facebook.com/TheMenofSin

--Twitter: twitter.com/CharityParkerso

www.ingramcontent.com/pod-product-compliance
Lightning Source LLC
Chambersburg PA
CBHW061251170626
46809CB00007B/2939